William Dean Howells

A Fearful Responsibility and Tonelli's Marriage

William Dean Howells

A Fearful Responsibility and Tonelli's Marriage

ISBN/EAN: 9783337817329

Printed in Europe, USA, Canada, Australia, Japan

Cover: Foto ©Andreas Hilbeck / pixelio.de

More available books at **www.hansebooks.com**

A FEARFUL
RESPONSIBILITY

AND

TONELLI'S MARRIAGE

BY

WILLIAM D. HOWELLS

Author's Edition

EDINBURGH
DAVID DOUGLAS, CASTLE STREET

1882

Edinburgh University Press:

T. AND A. CONSTABLE, PRINTERS TO HER MAJESTY.

Frederic Ernest Allsopp.

A FEARFUL RESPONSIBILITY.

A FEARFUL RESPONSIBILITY.

I.

EVERY loyal American who went abroad during the first years of our great war felt bound to make himself some excuse for turning his back on his country in the hour of her trouble. But when Owen Elmore sailed, no one else seemed to think that he needed excuse. All his friends said it was the best thing for him to do ; that he could have leisure and quiet over there, and would be able to go on with his work.

At the risk of giving a farcical effect to my narrative, I am obliged to confess that the work of which Elmore's friends spoke was a projected history of Venice. So many literary Americans have projected such a work that it may now fairly be regarded as

a national enterprise. Elmore was too obscure to have been announced in the usual
way by the newspapers as having this de-
sign ; but it was well known in his town
that he was collecting materials when his
professorship in the small inland college
with which he was connected lapsed through
the enlistment of nearly all the students.
The president became colonel of the college
regiment ; and in parting with Elmore,
while their boys waited on the campus without, he had said, "Now, Elmore, you must
go on with your history of Venice. Go to
Venice and collect your materials on the
spot. We 're coming through this all right.
Mr. Seward puts it at sixty days, but I 'll
give them six months to lay down their
arms, and we shall want you back at the
end of the year. Don't you have any com-
punctions about going. I know how you
feel ; but it is perfectly right for you to
keep out of it. Good-bye." They wrung
each other's hands for the last time,—the
president fell at Fort Donelson ; but now
Elmore followed him to the door, and when
he appeared there one of the boyish captains shouted, "Three cheers for Professor
Elmore !" and the president called for the

tiger, and led it, whirling his cap round his head.

Elmore went back to his study, sick at heart. It grieved and vexed him that even these had not thought that he should go to the war, and that his inward struggle on that point had been idle so far as others were concerned. He had been quite earnest in the matter; he had once almost volunteered as a private soldier : he had consulted his doctor, who sternly discouraged him. He would have been truly glad of any accident that forced him into the ranks ; but, as he used afterward to say, it was not his idea of soldiership to enlist for the hospital. At the distance of five hundred miles from the scene of hostilities, it was absurd to enter the Home Guard ; and, after all, there were, even at first, some selfish people who went into the army, and some unselfish people who kept out of it. Elmore's bronchitis was a disorder which active service would undoubtedly have aggravated ; as it was, he made a last effort to be of use to our Government as a bearer of despatches. Failing such an appointment, he submitted to expatriation as he best could ; and in Italy he fought for our cause against the

English, whom he found everywhere all but in arms against us.

He sailed, in fine, with a very fair conscience. "I should be perfectly at ease," he said to his wife, as the steamer dropped smoothly down to Sandy Hook, "if I were sure that I was not glad to be getting away."

"You are *not* glad," she answered.

"I don't know, I don't know," he said, with the weak persistence of a man willing that his wife should persuade him against his convictions ; "I wish that I felt certain of it."

"You are too sick to go to the war ; nobody expected you to go."

"I know that, and I can't say that I like it. As for being too sick, perhaps it's the part of a man to go if he dies on the way to the field. It would encourage the others," he added, smiling faintly.

She ignored the tint from Voltaire in replying : "Nonsense ! It would do no good at all. At any rate, it's too late now."

"Yes, it's too late now."

The sea-sickness which shortly followed formed a diversion from his accusing thoughts. Each day of the voyage removed them further, and with the preoccupations

of his first days in Europe, his travel to
Italy, and his preparations for a long sojourn in Venice, they had softened to a
pensive sense of self-sacrifice, which took a
warmer or a cooler tinge according as the
news from home was good or bad.

II.

HE lost no time in going to work in the Marcian Library, and he early applied to the Austrian authorities for leave to have transcripts made in the archives. The permission was negotiated by the American consul (then a young painter of the name of Ferris), who reported a mechanical facility on the part of the authorities,—as if, he said, they were used to obliging American historians of Venice. The foreign tyranny which cast a pathetic glamour over the romantic city had certainly not appeared to grudge such publicity as Elmore wished to give her heroic memories, though it was then at its most repressive period, and formed a check upon the whole life of the place. The tears were hardly yet dry in the despairing eyes that had seen the French fleet sail away from the Lido, after Solferino, without firing a shot in behalf of Venice; but Lombardy, the Duchies, the Sicilies, had all passed to Sardinia, and the Pope alone represented the old order of native despotism in Italy. At Venice the Germans seemed tranquilly awaiting the change which should destroy their system with the rest; and in the meantime there had occurred one of those impressive pauses, as notable in the lives of nations as of men, when, after the occurrence of great events, the forces of action and endurance seem to be gathering themselves against the stress of the future. The quiet was almost consciously a truce and not a peace; and this local calm had drawn into it certain elements that picturesquely and sentimentally heightened the charm of the place. It was a refuge for many exiled potentates and pretenders; the gondolier pointed out on the Grand Canal the palaces of the Count of Chambord, the Duchess of Parma, and the Infante of Spain; and one met these fallen princes in the squares and streets, bowing with distinct courtesy to any that chose to salute them. Every evening the Piazza San Marco was filled with the white coats of the Austrian officers, promenading to the exquisite military music which has ceased there for ever; the patrol clanked through the footways at

all hours of the night, and the lagoon heard
the cry of the sentinel from fort to fort, and
from gunboat to gunboat. Through all this
the demonstration of the patriots went on,
silent, ceaseless, implacable, annulling every
alien effort at gaiety, depopulating the theatres, and desolating the ancient holidays.

There was something very fine in this, as
a spectacle, Elmore said to his young wife,
and he had to admire the austere self-denial
of a people who would not suffer their tyrants
to see them happy ; but they secretly owned
to each other that it was fatiguing.   Soon
after coming to Venice they had made some
acquaintance among the Italians through Mr.
Ferris, and had early learned that the condition of knowing Venetians was not to know
Austrians.   It was easy and natural for them
to submit, theoretically.   As Americans, they
must respond to any impulse for freedom, and
certainly they could have no sympathy with
such a system as that of Austria.   By whatever was sacred in our own war upon slavery,
they were bound to abhor oppression in every
form.   But it was hard to make the application of their hatred to the amiable-looking
people whom they saw everywhere around
them in the quality of tyrants, especially

when their Venetian friends confessed that personally they liked the Austrians. Besides, if the whole truth must be told, they found that their friendship with the Italians was not always of the most penetrating sort, though it had a superficial intensity that for a while gave the effect of lasting cordiality. The Elmores were not quite able to decide whether the pause of feeling at which they arrived was through their own defect or not. Much was to be laid to the difference of race, religion, and education ; but something, they feared, to the personal vapidity of acquaintances whose meridional liveliness made them yawn, and in whose society they did not always find compensation for the sacrifices they made for it.

" But it is right," said Elmore. " It would be a sort of treason to associate with the Austrians. We owe it to the Venetians to let them see that our feelings are with them."

" Yes," said his wife pensively.

" And it is better for us, as Americans abroad, during this war, to be retired."

" Well, we are retired," said Mrs. Elmore.

" Yes, there is no doubt of that," he returned.

They laughed, and made what they could

B

of chance American acquaintances at the
caffès. Elmore had his history to occupy
him, and doubtless he could not understand
how heavy the time hung upon his wife's
hands. They went often to the theatre,
and every evening they went to the Piazza,
and ate an ice at Florian's. This was certainly amusement; and routine was so pleasant to his scholarly temperament that he
enjoyed merely that. He made a point of
admitting his wife as much as possible into
his intellectual life; he read her his notes as
fast as he made them, and he consulted her
upon the management of his theme, which,
as his research extended, he found so vast
that he was forced to decide upon a much
lighter treatment than he had at first intended. He had resolved upon a history
which should be presented in a series of bio-
graphical studies, and he was so much interested in this conclusion, and so charmed
with the advantages of the form as they developed themselves, that he began to lose the
sense of social dulness, and ceased to imagine
it in his wife.

A sort of indolence of the sensibilities, in
fact, enabled him to endure *ennui* that made
her frantic, and he was often deeply bored

without knowing it at the time, or without
a reasoned suffering. He suffered as a child
suffers, simply, almost ignorantly : it was
upon reflection that his nerves began to
quiver with retroactive anguish. He was
also able to idealise the situation when his
wife no longer even wished to do so. His
fancy cast a poetry about these Venetian
friends, whose conversation displayed the
occasional sparkle of Ollendorff-English on
a dark ground of lagoon-Italian, and whose
vivid smiling and gesticulation she wearied
herself in hospitable efforts to outdo. To his
eyes their historic past clothed them with
its interest, and the long patience of their
hope and hatred under foreign rule ennobled
them, while to hers they were too often only
tiresome visitors, whose powers of silence
and of eloquence were alike to be dreaded.
It did not console her as it did her husband
to reflect that they probably bored the Italians as much in their turn.   When a young
man, very sympathetic for literature and the
Americans, spent an evening, as it seemed
to her, in crying nothing but " Per Bácco ! "
she owned that she liked better his oppressor, who once came by chance, in the figure
of a young lieutenant, and who unbuckled his

wife, as he called his sword, and, putting her in a corner, sat up on a chair in the middle of the room and sang like a bird, and then told ghost stories. The songs were out of Heine, and they reminded her of her girlish enthusiasm for German. Elmore was troubled at the lieutenant's visit, and feared it would cost them all their Italian friends; but she said boldly that she did not care; and she never even tried to believe that the life they saw in Venice was comparable to that of their little college town at home, with its teas and picnics, and simple, easy social gaieties. There she had been a power in her way; she had entertained, and had helped to make some matches: but the Venetians ate nothing, and as for young people, they never saw each other but by stealth, and their matches were made by their parents on a money-basis. She could not adapt herself to this foreign life; it puzzled her, and her husband's conformity seemed to estrange them, as far as it went. It took away her spirit, and she grew listless and dull. Even the history began to lose its interest in her eyes; she doubted if the annals of such a people as she saw about her could ever be popular.

There were other things to make them melancholy in their exile. The war at home was going badly, where it was going at all. The letters now never spoke of any term to it; they expressed rather the dogged patience of the time when it seemed as if there could be no end, and indicated that the country had settled into shape about it, and was pushing forward its other affairs as if the war did not exist. Mrs. Elmore felt that the America which she had left had ceased to be. The letters were almost less a pleasure than a pain, but she always tore them open, and read them with eager unhappiness. There were miserable intervals of days and even weeks when no letters came, and when the Reuter telegrams in the Gazette of Venice dribbled their vitriolic news of Northern disaster through a few words or lines, and Galignani's long columns were filled with the hostile exultation and prophecy of the London press.

III.

THEY had passed eighteen months of this
sort of life in Venice when one day a
letter dropped into it which sent a thousand
ripples over its stagnant surface. Mrs.
Elmore read it first to herself, with gasps
and cries of pleasure and astonishment,
which did not divert her husband from the
perusal of some notes he had made the day
before, and had brought to the breakfast-
table with the intention of amusing her.
When she flattened it out over his notes,
and exacted his attention, he turned an unwilling and lack-lustre eye upon it ; then he
looked up at her.

" Did you expect she would come ?" he
asked, in ill-masked dismay.

" I don't suppose they had any idea of it
at first. When Sue wrote me that Lily had
been studying too hard, and had to be taken
out of school, I said that I wished she could
come over and pay us a visit. But I don't

believe they dreamed of letting her—Sue says so—till the Mortons' coming seemed too good a chance to be lost. I am so glad of it, Owen ! You know how much they have always done for me ; and here is a chance now to pay a little of it back."

" What in the world shall we do with her ?" he asked.

" Do ? Everything ! Why, Owen," she urged, with pathetic recognition of his coldness, " she is Susy Stevens's own sister !"

" Oh, yes—yes," he admitted.

" And it was Susy who brought us together !"

" Why, of course."

" And oughtn't you to be glad of the opportunity ?"

" I *am* glad—*very* glad."

" It will be a relief to you instead of a care. She's such a bright, intelligent girl that we can both sympathise with your work, and you won't have to go round with me all the time, and I can matronise her myself."

" I see, I see," Elmore replied, with scarcely abated seriousness. " Perhaps, if she is coming here for her health, she won't need much matronising."

"Oh, pshaw! She'll be well enough for *that!* She's overdone a little at school. I shall take good care of her, I can tell you; and I shall make her have a real good time. It's quite flattering of Susy to trust her to us, so far away, and I shall write and tell her we both think so."

"Yes," said Elmore, "it's a fearful responsibility."

There are instances of the persistence of husbands in certain moods or points of view on which even wheedling has no effect. The wise woman perceives that in these cases she must trust entirely to the softening influences of time, and as much as possible she changes the subject; or if this is impossible she may hope something from presenting a still worse aspect of the affair. Mrs. Elmore said, in lifting the letter from the table:
"If she sailed the 3d in the 'City of Timbuctoo,' she will be at Queenstown on the 12th or 13th, and we shall have a letter from her by Wednesday saying when she will be at Genoa. That's as far as the Mortons can bring her, and there's where we must meet her."

"Meet her in Genoa! How?"

"By going there for her," replied Mrs.

Elmore, as if this were the simplest thing in
the world. " I have never seen Gt noa."

Elmore now tacitly abandoned himself to
his fate. His wife continued : " I needn't
take anything. Merely run on, and right
back."

" When must we go ?" he asked.

" I don't know yet ; but we shall have a
letter to-morrow. Don't worry on my account, Owen. Her coming won't be a bit of
care to me. It will give me something to
do and to think about, and it will be a pleasure all the time to know that it 's for Susy
Stevens. And I shall like the companion-
ship."

Elmore looked at his wife in surprise, for
it had not occurred to him before that with
his company she could desire any other com-
panionship. He desired none but hers, and
when he was about his work he often thought
of her. He supposed that at these moments
she thought of him, and found society, as he
did, in such thoughts. But he was not a
jealous or exacting man, and he said nothing.
His treatment of the approaching visit from
Susy Stevens's sister had not been enthusi-
astic, but a spark had kindled his imagination, and it burned warmer and brighter as

the days went by. He found a charm in the
thought of having this fresh young life here
in his charge, and of teaching the girl to live
into the great and beautiful history of the
city ; there was still much of the school-
master in him, and he intended to make her
sojourn an education to her ; and as a literary man he hoped for novel effects from her
mind upon material which he was above all
trying to set in a new light before himself.

When the time had arrived for them to go
and meet Miss Mayhew at Genoa, he was
more than reconciled to the necessity. But
at the last moment, Mrs. Elmore had one of
her old attacks. What these attacks were I
find myself unable to specify, but as every
lady has an old attack of some kind, I may
safely leave their precise nature to conjecture.   It is enough that they were of a
nervous character, that they were accom-
panied with headache, and that they prostrated her for several days. During their
continuance she required the active sympathy and constant presence of her husband,
whose devotion was then exemplary, and
brought up long arrears of indebtedness in
that way.

"Well, what shall we do ?" he asked, as

he sank into a chair beside the lounge on which Mrs. Elmore lay, her eyes closed, and a slice of lemon placed on each of her throbbing temples with the effect of a new sort of blinders. "Shall I go alone for her?"

She gave his hand the kind of convulsive clutch that signified, "Impossible for you to leave me."

He reflected. "The Mortons will be pushing on to Leghorn, and somebody *must* meet her. How would it do for Mr. Hoskins to go?"

Mrs. Elmore responded with a clutch tantamount to "Horrors! How could you think of such a thing?"

"Well, then," he said, "the only thing we can do is to send a *valet de place* for her. We can send old Gazzi. He's the incarnation of respectability; five francs a day and his expenses will buy all the virtues of him. She'll come as safely with him as with me."

Mrs. Elmore had applied a vividly thoughtful pressure to her husband's hand; she now released it in token of assent, and he rose.

"But don't be gone long," she whispered.

On his way to the caffè which Gazzi frequented, Elmore fell in with the consul.

By this time a change had taken place in

the consular office. Mr. Ferris, some months
before, had suddenly thrown up his charge
and gone home ; and after the customary
interval of ship-chandler, the California
sculptor, Hoskins, had arrived out, with his
commission in his pocket, and had set up his
allegorical figure of "The Pacific Slope" in
the room where Ferris had painted his too
metaphysical conception of "A Venetian
Priest."   Mrs. Elmore had never liked
Ferris ; she thought him cynical and opin-
ionated, and she believed that he had not
behaved quite well towards a young American lady,—a Miss Vervain, who had stayed
a while in Venice with her mother.   She
was glad to have him go ; but she could
not admire Mr. Hoskins, who, however good-
hearted, was too hopelessly Western.   He
had had part of one foot shot away in the
nine months' service, and walked with a
limp that did him honour ; and he knew as
much of a consul's business as any of the
authors or artists with whom it is the tradi-
tion to fill that office at Venice.   Besides, he
was at least a fellow-American, and Elmore
could not forbear telling him the trouble he
was in : a young girl coming from their town
in America as far as Genoa with friends, and

expecting to be met there by the Elmores, with whom she was to pass some months ; Mrs. Elmore utterly prostrated by one of her old attacks, and he unable to leave her, or to take her with him to Genoa ; the friends with whom Miss Mayhew travelled unable to bring her to Venice ; she, of course, unable to come alone. The case deepened and darkened in Elmore's view as he unfolded it.

" Why," cried the consul sympathetically, " if I could leave my post I 'd go ! "

" Oh, thank you ! " cried Elmore eagerly, remembering his wife. " I couldn't think of letting you."

" Look here ! " said the consul, taking an official letter, with the seal broken, from his pocket. " This is the first time I couldn't have left my post without distinct advantage to the public interests, since I 've been here. But with this letter from Turin, telling me to be on the look-out for the ' Alabama,' I couldn't go to Genoa even to meet a young lady. The Austrians have never recognised the rebels as belligerents : if she enters the port of Venice, all I 've got to do is to require the deposit of her papers with me, and then I should like to see her get out again. I *should* like to capture her. Of course, I

don't mean Miss Mayhew," said the consul,
recognising the double sense in which his
language could be taken.

"It would be a great thing for you," said
Elmore,—"a *great* thing."

"Yes, it would set me up in my own eyes,
and stop that infernal clatter inside about
going over and taking a hand again."

"Yes," Elmore assented, with a twinge of
the old shame. "I didn't know you had it
too."

"If I could capture the 'Alabama,' I
could afford to let the other fellows fight it
out."

"I congratulate you with all my heart,"
said Elmore sadly, and he walked in silence
beside the consul.

"Well," said the latter, with a laugh at
Elmore's pensive rapture. "I'm as much
obliged to you as if I *had* captured her. I'll
go up to the Piazza with you, and see Gazzi."

The affair was easily arranged ; Gazzi was
made to feel by the consul's intervention
that the shield of American sovereignty had
been extended over the young girl whom he
was to escort from Genoa, and two days
later he arrived with her. Mrs. Elmore's
attack now was passing off, and she was well

enough to receive Miss Mayhew half-recum-
bent on the sofa where she had been prone
till her arrival. It was pretty to see her
fond greeting of the girl, and her joy in her
presence as they sat down for the first long
talk; and Elmore realised, even in his
dreamy withdrawal, how much the bright,
active spirit of his wife had suffered merely
in the restriction of her English. Now it
was not only English they spoke, but that
American variety of the language of which
I hope we shall grow less and less ashamed;
and not only this, but their parlance was
characterised by local turns and accents,
which all came welcomely back to Mrs.
Elmore, together with those still more
intimate inflections which belonged to her
own particular circle of friends in the little
town of Patmos, N. Y. Lily Mayhew was
of course not of her own set, being five or
six years younger; but women, more easily
than men, ignore the disparities of age
between themselves and their juniors; and
in Susy Stevens's absence it seemed a sort
of tribute to her to establish her sister in the
affection which Mrs. Elmore had so long
cherished. Their friendship had been of
such a thoroughly trusted sort on both sides

that Mrs. Stevens (the memorably brilliant
Sue Mayhew in her girlish days) had felt
perfectly free to act upon Mrs. Elmore's
invitation to let Lily come out to her ; and
here the child was, as much at home as if
she had just walked into Mrs. Elmore's
parlour out of her sister's house in Patmos.

IV.

THEY briefly despatched the facts relating to Miss Mayhew's voyage, and her journey to Genoa, and came as quickly as they could to all those things which Mrs. Elmore was thirsting to learn about the town and its people. "Is it much changed? I suppose it is," she sighed. "The war changes everything."

"Oh, you don't notice the war much," said Miss Mayhew. "But Patmos *is* gay,— perfectly delightful. We've got one of the camps there now ; and *such* times as the girls have with the officers ! We have lots of fun getting up things for the Sanitary. Hops on the parade-ground at the camp, and going out to see the prisoners,—you never saw such a place."

" The prisoners ?" murmured Mrs. Elmore.

" Why, *yes !* " cried Lily, with a gay laugh. " Didn't you know that we had a prison-camp too? Some of the Southerners look

c

real nice. I pitied them," she added, with unabated gaiety.

"Your sister wrote to me," said Mrs. Elmore; "but I couldn't realise it, I suppose, and so I forgot it."

"Yes," pursued Lily, "and Frank Halsey's in command. You would never know by the way he walks that he had a cork leg. Of course he can't dance, though, poor fellow. He's pale, and he's perfectly fascinating. So's Dick Burton, with his empty sleeve; he's one of the recruiting officers, and there's nobody so popular with the girls. You can't think how funny it is, Professor Elmore, to see the old college buildings used for barracks. Dick says it's much livelier than it was when he was a student there."

"I suppose it must be," dreamily assented the professor. "Does he find plenty of volunteers?"

"Well, you know," the young girl explained, "that the old style of volunteering is all over."

"No, I didn't know it."

"Yes. It's the bounties now that they rely upon, and they do say that it will come to the draft very soon, now. Some of the young men have gone to Canada. But

everybody despises *them.* Oh, Mrs. Elmore,
I should think you 'd be *so* glad to have the
professor off here, and honourably out of the
way !"

" I 'm *dis*honourably out of the way ; I can
never forgive myself for not going to the
war," said Elmore.

" Why, how ridiculous !" cried Lily.
" Nobody feels that way about it *now !* As
Dick Burton says, we 've come down to business. I tell you, when you see arms and
legs off in every direction, and women going
about in black, you don't feel that it 's such
a romantic thing any more. There are mighty
few engagements now, Mrs. Elmore, when
a regiment sets off; no presentation of re-
volvers in the town hall ; and some of the
widows have got married again ; and that I
don't think *is* right. But what can they do,
poor things ? You remember Tom Friar's
widow, Mrs. Elmore ?"

" Tom Friar's *widow !* Is Tom Friar
dead ?"

" Why, of course ! One of the first. I
think it was Ball's Bluff. Well, *she 's* mar-
·ried. But she married his cousin, and as
Dick Burton says, that isn't so bad. Isn't it
awful, Mrs. Clapp 's losing *all* her boys,—all

five of them? It does seem to bear too hard on *some* families. And then, when you see every one of those six Armstrongs going through without a scratch !"

" I suppose," said Elmore, "that business is at a standstill. The streets must look rather dreary."

"*Business* at a standstill !" exclaimed Lily. " What *has* Sue been writing you all this time? Why, there never was such prosperity in Patmos before! Everybody is making money, and people that you wouldn't hardly speak to a year ago are giving parties and inviting the old college families. You ought to see the residences and business blocks going up all over the place. I don't suppose you would know Patmos now. You remember George Fenton, Mrs. Elmore?"

" Mr. Haskell's clerk ?"

" Yes. Well, he's made a fortune out of an army contract; and he's going to marry— the engagement came out just before I left —Bella Stearns."

At these words Mrs. Elmore sat upright, —the only posture in which the fact could be imagined. " Lily !"

" Oh, I can tell you these are gay times in America," triumphed the young girl. She now put her hand to her mouth and hid a yawn.

"You're sleepy," said Mrs. Elmore. "Well, you know the way to your room. You'll find everything ready there, and I shall let you go alone. You shall commence being at home at once."

"Yes, I *am* sleepy," assented Lily; and she promptly said her good-nights and vanished; though a keener eye than Elmore's might have seen that her promptness had a colour—or say light—of hesitation in it.

But he only walked up and down the room, after she was gone, in unheedful distress. "Gay times in America! Good heavens! Is the child utterly heartless, Celia, or is she merely obtuse?"

"She certainly isn't at all like Sue," sighed Mrs. Elmore, who had not had time to formulate Lily's defence. "But she's excited now, and a little off her balance. She'll be different to-morrow. Besides, all America seems changed, and the people with it. We shouldn't have noticed it if we had stayed there, but we feel it after this absence."

"I never realised it before, as I did from her babble! The letters have told us the same thing, but they were like the histories of other times. Camps, prisoners, barracks, mutilation, widowhood, death, sudden gains, social upheavals, — it is the old, hideous story of war come true of our day and country. It's terrible!"

"She will miss the excitement," said Mrs. Elmore. "I don't know exactly what we shall do with her. Of course, she can't expect the attentions she's been used to in Patmos, with those young men."

Elmore stopped, and stared at his wife. "What do you mean, Celia?"

"We don't go into society at all, and she doesn't speak Italian. How shall we amuse her?"

"Well, upon my word, I don't know that we're obliged to provide her amusement! Let her amuse herself. Let her take up some branch of study, or of—of—research, and get something besides 'fun' into her head, if possible." He spoke boldly, but his wife's question had unnerved him, for he had a soft heart, and liked people about him to be happy. "We can show her the objects of interest. And there are the theatres," he added.

"Yes, that is true," said Mrs. Elmore.

"We can both go about with her. I will just peep in at her now, and see if she has everything she wants." She rose from her sofa and went to Lily's room, whence she did not return for nearly three quarters of an hour. By this time Elmore had got out his notes, and, in their transcription and classification, had fallen into forgetfulness of his troubles. His wife closed the door behind her, and said in a low voice, little above a whisper, as she sank very quietly into a chair, " Well, it has all come out, Owen."

"What has all come out?" he asked, looking up stupidly.

"I knew that she had something on her mind, by the way she acted. And you saw her give me that look as she went out?"

"No—no, I didn't. What look was it? She looked sleepy."

"She looked terribly, terribly excited, and as if she would like to say something to me. That was the reason I said I would let her go to her room alone."

"Oh !"

"Of course she would have felt awfully if I had gone straight off with her. So I waited. It *may* never come to anything in the world, and I don't suppose it will ; but it's quite enough to account for everything you saw in her."

"I didn't see anything in her,—that was the difficulty. But what is it—what is it, Celia? You know how I hate these delays."

"Why, I'm not sure that I need tell you, Owen; and yet I suppose I had better. It will be safer," said Mrs. Elmore, nursing her mystery to the last, enjoying it for its own sake, and dreading it for its effect upon her husband. "I suppose you will think your troubles are beginning pretty early," she suggested.

"Is it a trouble?"

"Well, I don't know that it is. If it comes to the very worst, I daresay that every one wouldn't call it a trouble."

Elmore threw himself back in his chair in an attitude of endurance. "What would the worst be?"

"Why, it's no use even to discuss that, for it's perfectly absurd to suppose that it could ever come to that. But the case," added Mrs. Elmore, perceiving that further delay was only further suffering for her husband, and that any fact would now probably fall far short of his apprehensions, "is

simply this, and I don't know that it amounts
to anything; but at Peschiera, just before
the train started, she looked out of the
window, and saw a splendid officer walking
up and down and smoking; and before she
could draw back he must have seen her, for
he threw away his cigar instantly, and got
into the same compartment. He talked a
while in German with an old gentleman
who was there, and then he spoke in Italian
with Gazzi; and afterwards, when he heard
her speaking English with Gazzi, he joined in.
I don't know how he came to join in at first,
and she doesn't, either; but it seems that he
knew some English, and he began speaking.
He was very tall and handsome and distin-
guished-looking, and a *perfect* gentleman in
his manners; and she says that she saw
Gazzi looking rather queer, but he didn't say
anything, and so she kept on talking. She
told him at once that she was an American, and that she was coming here to stay
with friends; and, as he was very curious
about America, she told him all she could
think of. It did her good to talk about
home, for she had been feeling a little blue
at being so far away from everybody. Now,
I don't see any harm in it; do you, Owen?"

" It isn't according to the custom here ; but we needn't care for that. Of course it was imprudent."

"Of course," Mrs. Elmore admitted. " The officer was very polite ; and when he found that she was from America, it turned out that he was a *great* sympathiser with the North, and that he had a brother in our army. Don't you think that was nice ?"

" Probably some mere soldier of fortune, with no heart in the cause," said Elmore.

" And very likely he has no brother there, as I told Lily. He told her he was coming to Padua ; but when they reached Padua, he came right on to Venice. That *shows* you couldn't place any dependence upon what he said. He said he expected to be put under arrest for it ; but he didn't care,—he was coming. Do you believe they'll put him under arrest ?"

" I don't know—I don't know," said Elmore, in a voice of grief and apprehension, which might well have seemed anxiety for the officer's liberty.

" I told her it was one of his jokes. He was very funny, and kept her laughing the whole way, with his broken English and his witty little remarks. She says he's just dying to go to America. Who do you suppose it can be, Owen?"

"How should I know? We've no acquaintance among the Austrians," groaned Elmore.

"That's what I told Lily. She's no idea of the state of things here, and she was quite horrified. But she says he was a perfect gentleman in everything. He belongs to the engineer corps,—that's one of the highest branches of the service, he told her,—and he gave her his card."

"Gave her his card!"

Mrs. Elmore had it in the hand which she had been keeping in her pocket, and she now suddenly produced it; and Elmore read the name and address of Ernst von Ehrhardt, Captain of the Royal-Imperial Engineers, Peschiera. "She says she knows he wanted hers, but she didn't offer to give it to him; and he didn't ask her where she was going, or anything."

"He knew that he could get her address from Gazzi for ten soldi as soon as her back was turned," said Elmore cynically. "What then?"

"Why, he said—and this is the only really bold thing he *did* do—that he must see her

again, and that he should stay over a day in
Venice in hopes of meeting her at the theatre
or somewhere."

"It 's a piece of high-handed impudence !"
cried Elmore. "Now, Celia, you see what
these people are! Do you wonder that the
Italians hate them ?"

"You 've often said they only hate their
system."

"The Austrians are part of their system.
He thinks he can take any liberty with us
because he is an Austrian officer! Lily
must not stir out of the house to-morrow."

"She will be too tired to do so," said Mrs.
Elmore.

"And if he molests us further, I will
appeal to the consul." Elmore began to
walk up and down the room again.

"Well, I don't know whether you could
call it *molesting*, exactly," suggested Mrs.
Elmore.

"What do you mean, Celia? Do you
suppose that she — she — encouraged this
officer ?"

"Owen ! It was all in the simplicity and
innocence of her heart !

"Well, then, that she wishes to see him
again ?"

"Certainly not! But that's no reason why we should be rude about it."

"Rude about it? How? Is simply avoiding him rudeness? Is proposing to protect ourselves from his impertinence rudeness?"

"No. And if you can't see the matter for yourself, Owen, I don't know how any one is to make you."

"Why, Celia, one would think that you approved of this man's behaviour,—that *you* wished her to meet him again! You understand what the consequences would be if we received this officer. You know how all the Venetians would drop us, and we should have no acquaintances here outside of the army."

"Who has asked you to receive him, Owen? And as for the Italians dropping us, that doesn't frighten me. But what could he do if he did meet her again? She needn't look at him. She says he is very intelligent, and that he has read a great many English books, though he doesn't speak it very well, and that he knows more about the war than she does. But of course she won't go out to-morrow. All that I hate is that we should seem to be frightened into staying at home."

" She needn't stay in on his account. You
said she would be too tired to go out."

" I see by the scattering way you talk,
Owen, that your mind isn't on the subject,
and that you 're anxious to get back to your
work. I won't keep you."

" Celia, Celia ! Be fair, now !" cried
Elmore. " You know very well that I 'm
only too deeply interested in this matter,
and that I 'm not likely to get back to my
work to-night, at least. What is it you
wish me to do ? "

Mrs. Elmore considered a while. " I don't
wish you to do anything," she returned, plac-
ably. " Of course, you 're perfectly right in
not choosing to let an acquaintance begun
in that way go any further. We shouldn't
at home, and we shan't here. But I don't
wish you to think that Lily has been imprudent, under the circumstances. She doesn't
know that it was anything out of the way,
but she happened to do the best that any
one could. Of course, it was very exciting
and very romantic ; girls like such things,
and there 's no reason they shouldn't. We
must manage," added Mrs. Elmore, " so that
she shall see that we appreciate her conduct,
and trust in her entirely. I wouldn't do

anything to wound her pride or self-confidence. I would rather send her out alone to-morrow."

"Of course," said Elmore.

"And if I were with her when she met him, I believe I should leave it entirely to her how to behave."

"Well," said Elmore, "you 're not likely to be put to the test. He 'll hardly force his way into the house, and she isn't going out."

"No," said Mrs. Elmore. She added, after a silence, "I 'm trying to think whether I 've ever seen him in Venice ; he 's here often. But there are so many tall officers with fair complexions and English beards. I *should* like to know how he looks ! She said he was very aristocratic-looking."

"Yes, it 's a fine type," said Elmore. "They 're all nobles, I believe."

"But after all, they 're no better-looking than our boys, who come up out of nothing."

"Ours are Americans," said Elmore.

"And they are the best husbands, as I told Lily."

Elmore looked at his wife, as she turned dreamily to leave the room ; but since the conversation had taken this impersonal turn

he would not say anything to change its
complexion. A conjecture vaguely taking
shape in his mind resolved itself to nothing
again, and left him with only the ache of
something unascertained.

V.

IN the morning Lily came to breakfast as blooming as a rose. The sense of her simple, fresh, wholesome loveliness might have pierced even the indifference of a man to whom there was but one pretty woman in the world, and who had lived since their marriage as if his wife had absorbed her whole sex into herself; this deep, unconscious constancy was a noble trait in him, but it is not so rare in men as women would have us believe. For Elmore, Miss Mayhew merely pervaded the place in her finer way, as the flowers on the table did, as the sweet butter, the new eggs, and the morning's French bread did; he looked at her with a perfectly serene ignorance of her piquant face, her beautiful eyes and abundant hair, and her trim, straight figure. But his wife exulted in every particular of her charm, and was as generously glad of it as if it were her own; as women are when they are sure

D

that the charm of others has no designs. The ladies twittered and laughed together, and as he was a man without small talk, he soon dropped out of the conversation into a reverie, from which he found himself presently extracted by a question from his wife.

"We had better go in a gondola, hadn't we, Owen?" She seemed to be, as she put this, trying to look something into him. He, on his part, tried his best to make out her meaning, but failed.

He simply asked, "Where? Are you going out?"

"Yes. Lily has some shopping she *must* do. I think we can get it at Pazienti's in San Polo."

Again she tried to pierce him with her meaning. It seemed to him a sudden advance from the position she had taken the night before in regard to Miss Mayhew's not going out ; but he could not understand his wife's look, and he feared to misinterpret if he opposed her going. He decided that she wished him for some reason to oppose the gondola, so he said, "I think you'd better walk, if Lily isn't too tired."

"Oh, *I'm* not tired at all !" she cried.

"I can go with you, in that direction, on my way to the library," he added.

"Well, that will be very nice," said Mrs. Elmore, discontinuing her look, and leaving her husband with an uneasy sense of wantonly assumed responsibility.

"She can step into the Frari a moment, and see those tombs," he said. "I think it will amuse her."

Lily broke into a laugh. "Is that the way you amuse yourselves in Venice?" she asked; and Mrs. Elmore hastened to reassure her.

"That's the way Mr. Elmore amuses himself. You know his history makes every bit of the past fascinating to him."

"Oh, yes, that history! Everybody is looking out for that," said Lily.

"Is it possible," said Elmore, with a pensive sarcasm in which an agreeable sense of flattery lurked, "that people still remember me and my history?"

"Yes, indeed!" cried Miss Mayhew. "Frank Halsey was talking about it the night before I left. He couldn't seem to understand why I should be coming to you at Venice, because he said it was a history of Florence you were writing. It isn't, is it?

You must be getting pretty near the end of it, Professor Elmore."

" I 'm getting pretty near the beginning," said Elmore sadly.

"It must be hard writing histories; they 're so awfully hard to read," said Lily innocently. " Does it interest you ?" she asked, with unaffected compassion.

" Yes," he said, " far more than it will ever interest anybody else."

" Oh, I don't believe that !" she cried sweetly, seizing the occasion to get in a little compliment.

Mrs. Elmore sat silent, while things were thus going against Miss Mayhew, and perhaps she was then meditating the stroke by which she restored the balance to her own favour as soon as she saw her husband alone after breakfast. " Well. Owen," she said, " you 've done it now."

" Done what ?" he demanded.

" Oh, nothing, perhaps !" she answered, while she got on her things for the walk with unusual gaiety ; and, with the consciousness of unknown guilt depressing him, he followed the ladies upon their errand, subdued, distraught, but gradually forgetting his sin, as he forgot everything but his

history. His wife hated to see him so miserable, and whispered at the shop-door where
they parted, "Don't be troubled, Owen ! I
didn't mean anything."

"By what?"

"Oh, if you've forgotten, never mind !"
she cried ; and she and Miss Mayhew disappeared within.

It was two hours later when he next saw
them, after he had turned over the book he
wished to see, and had found the passage
which would enable him to go on with his
work for the rest of the day at home. He
was fitting his key into the house-door when
he happened to look up the little street toward the bridge that led into it, and there,
defined against the sky on the level of the
bridge, he saw Mrs. Elmore and Miss Mayhew receiving the adieux of a distinguished-
looking man in the Austrian uniform. The
officer had brought his heels together in the
conventional manner, and with his cap in his
right hand, while his left rested on the hilt
of his sword, and pressed it down, he was
bowing from the hips. Once, twice, and he
was gone.

The ladies came down the *calle* with rapid
steps and flushed faces, and Elmore let them

in. His wife whispered as she brushed by his elbow, "I want to speak with you instantly, Owen. Well, now!" she added, when they were alone in their own room and she had shut the door, "what do you say *now?*"

"What do *I* say now, Celia?" retorted Elmore, with just indignation. "It seems to me that it is for *you* to say something—or nothing."

"Why, you brought it on us."

Elmore merely glanced at his wife, and did not speak, for this passed all force of language.

"Didn't you see me looking at you when I spoke of going out in a gondola, at breakfast?"

"Yes."

"What did you suppose I meant?"

"I didn't know."

"When I was trying to make you understand that if we took a gondola we could go and come without being seen! Lily *had* to do her shopping. But if you chose to run off on some interpretation of your own, was *I* to blame, I should like to know? No, indeed! You won't get me to admit it, Owen."

Elmore continued inarticulate, but he made a low, miserable sibillation between his set teeth.

"Such presumption, such perfect audacity I never saw in my life !" cried Mrs. Elmore, fleetly changing the subject in her own mind, and leaving her husband to follow her as he could. "It was outrageous !" Her words were strong, but she did not really look affronted ; and it is hard to tell what sort of liberty it is that affronts a woman. It seems to depend a great deal upon the person who takes the liberty.

"That was the man, I suppose," said Elmore quietly.

"Yes, Owen," answered his wife, with beautiful candour, "it was." Seeing that he remained unaffected by her display of this virtue, she added, "Don't you think he was very handsome ?"

"I couldn't judge, at such a distance."

"Well, he is perfectly splendid. And I don't want you to think he was disrespectful at all. He wasn't. He was everything that was delicate and deferential."

"Did you ask him to walk home with you ?"

Mrs. Elmore remained speechless for some

moments. Then she drew a long breath, and said firmly: "If you won't interrupt me with gratuitous insults, Owen, I will tell you all about it, and then perhaps you will be ready to do me *justice*. I ask nothing more." She waited for his contrition, but proceeded without it, in a somewhat meeker strain: "Lily couldn't get her things at Pazienti's, and we had to go to the Merceria for them. Then of course the nearest way home was through St. Mark's Square. I made Lily go on the Florian side, so as to avoid the officers who were sitting at the Quadri, and we had got through the square and past San Moïsè, as far as the Stadt Gratz. I had never thought of how the officers frequented the Stadt Gratz, but there we met a most magnificent creature, and I had just said, 'What a splendid officer!' when she gave a sort of stop and he gave a sort of stop, and bowed very low, and she whispered, 'It's my officer.' I didn't dream of his joining us, and I don't think he did, at first; but after he took a second look at Lily, it really seemed as if he couldn't help it. He asked if he might join us, and I didn't say anything."

"Didn't say anything!"

" *No!* How could I refuse, in so many words ? And I was frightened and confused, any way. He asked if we were going to the music in the Giardini Pubblici ; and I said No, that Miss Mayhew was not going into society in Venice, but was merely here for her health. That's all there is of it. Now do you blame me, Owen ?"

" No."

" Do you blame her ?"

" No."

" Well, I don't see how *he* was to blame."

" The transaction was a little irregular, but it was highly creditable to all parties concerned."

Mrs. Elmore grew still meeker under this irony. Indignation and censure she would have known how to meet ; but his quiet perplexed her ; she did not know what might not be coming. "Lily scarcely spoke to him," she pursued, " and I was very cold. I spoke to him in German."

" Is German a particularly repellent tongue ?"

" No. But I was determined he should get no hold upon us. He was very polite and very respectful, as I said, but I didn't give him an atom of encouragement ; I saw that he was dying to be asked to call, but I parted from him very stiffly."

"Is it possible ?"

"Owen, what *is* there so wrong about it all ? He's clearly fascinated with her ; and as the matter stood, he had no hope of seeing her or speaking with her except on the street. Perhaps he didn't know it was wrong,—or didn't realise it."

"I dare say."

"What else could the poor fellow have done ? There he was ! He had stayed over a day, and laid himself open to arrest, on the bare chance—one in a hundred—of seeing Lily ; and when he did see her, what was he to do ?"

"Obviously, to join her and walk home with her."

"You are too bad, Owen !   Suppose it had been one of our own poor boys ?   He *looked* like an American."

"He didn't behave like one. One of 'our own poor boys,' as you call them, would have been as far as possible from thrusting himself upon you. He would have had too much reverence for you, too much self-respect, too much pride."

"What has pride to do with such things,

my dear? I think he acted very naturally.
He acted upon impulse. I'm sure you're
always crying out against the restraints and
conventionalities between young people, over
here; and now, when a European *does* do
a simple, unaffected thing"—

Elmore made a gesture of impatience.
"This fellow has presumed upon your being
Americans—on your ignorance of the customs
here—to take a liberty that he would not
have dreamed of taking with Italian or German ladies. He has shown himself no gentleman."

"Now there you are very much mistaken,
Owen. That's what I thought when Lily
first told me about his speaking to her in
the cars, and I was very much prejudiced
against him; but when I saw him to-day, I
must say that I felt that I had been wrong.
He *is* a gentleman; but—he is desperate."

"Oh, indeed!"

"Yes," said Mrs. Elmore, shrinking a
little under her husband's sarcastic tone.
"Why, Owen," she pleaded, "can't you see
anything romantic in it?"

"I see nothing but a vulgar impertinence
in it. I see it from his standpoint as an adventure to be bragged of and laughed over

at the mess-table and the caffè. I 'm going
to put a stop to it."

Mrs. Elmore looked daunted and a little
bewildered. "Well, Owen," she said, "I
put the affair entirely in your hands."

Elmore never could decide upon just what
theory his wife had acted; he had to rest
upon the fact, already known to him, of her
perfect truth and conscientiousness, and his
perception that even in a good woman the
passion for manœuvring and intrigue may
approach the point at which men commit
forgery. He now saw her quelled and sub-
missive; but he was by no means sure that
she looked at the affair as he did, or that she
voluntarily acquiesced.

"All that I ask is that you won't do anything that you 'll regret afterward. And
as for putting a stop to it, I fancy it 's put
a stop to already. He 's going back to
Peschiera this afternoon, and that 'll probably be the last of him."

"Very well," said Elmore, "if that is the
last of him, I ask nothing better. I certainly
have no wish to take any steps in the
matter."

But he went out of the house very unhappy and greatly perplexed. He thought

at first of going to the Stadt Gratz, where
Captain Ehrhardt was probably staying for
the tap of Vienna beer peculiar to that
hostelry, and of inquiring him out, and re-
questing him to discontinue his attentions;
but this course, upon reflection, was less
high-handed than comported with his present mood, and he turned aside to seek
advice of his consul. He found Mr. Hoskins
in the best humour for backing his quarrel.
He had just received a second despatch from
Turin, stating that the rumour of the approaching visit of the "Alabama" was un-
founded; and he was thus left with a force
of unexpended belligerence on his hands
which he was glad to contribute to the
defence of Mr. Elmore's family from the
pursuit of this Austrian officer.

"This is a very simple affair, Mr. Elmore,"
—he usually said "Elmore," but in his
haughty frame of mind, he naturally threw
something more of state into their inter-
course,—"a very simple affair, fortunately.
All that I have to do is to call on the military
governor, and state the facts of the case, and
this fellow will get his orders quietly and
definitively. This war has sapped our influence in Europe,—there's no doubt of it;

but I think it's a pity if an American family living in this city can't be safe from molestation ; and if it can't I want to know the reason why."

This language was very acceptable to Elmore, and he thanked the consul. At the same time he felt his own resentment moderated, and he said, " I'm willing to let the matter rest if he goes away this afternoon."

" Oh, of course," Hoskins assented, " if he clears out, that's the end of it. I'll look in to-morrow, and see how you're getting along."

" Don't—don't give them the impression that I've—profited by your kindness," suggested Elmore at parting.

" You haven't yet. I only hope you may have the chance."

" Thank you ; I don't think *I* do."

Elmore took a long walk, and returned home tranquillised and clarified as to the situation. Since it could be terminated without difficulty and without scandal in the way Hoskins had explained, he was not unwilling to see a certain poetry in it. He could not repress a degree of sympathy with the bold young fellow who had overstepped the conventional proprieties in the ardour of a romantic impulse, and he could see how this very boldness, while it had a terror, would have a charm for a young girl. There was no necessity, except for the purpose of holding Mrs. Elmore in check, to look at it in an ugly light. Perhaps the officer had inferred from Lily's innocent frankness of manner that this sort of approach was permissible with Americans, and was not amusing himself with the adventure, but was in love in earnest. Elmore could allow himself this view of a case which he had so completely in his own hands; and he was sensible of a sort of pleasure in the novel responsibility thrown upon him. Few men at his age were called upon to stand in the place of a parent to a young girl, to intervene in her affairs, and to decide who was and who was not a proper person to pretend to her acquaintance.

Feeling so secure in his right, he rebelled against the restraint he had proposed to himself, and at dinner he invited the ladies to go to the opera with him. He chose to show himself in public with them, and to check any impression that they were without due protection. As usual, the pit was full of officers, and between the acts they all rose, as usual, and faced the boxes, which they

perused through their *lorgnettes* till the bell
rang for the curtain to rise. But Mrs. Elmore, having touched his arm to attract his
notice, instructed him, by a slow turning of
her head, that Captain Ehrhardt was not
there. After that he undoubtedly breathed
freer, and in the relaxation from his sense of
bravado, he enjoyed the last acts of the opera
more than the first. Miss Mayhew showed
no disappointment; and she bore herself
with so much grace and dignity, and yet
so evidently impressed every one with her
beauty, that he was proud of having her in
charge. He began himself to see that she
was pretty.

VI.

THE next day was Sunday, and in going to church they missed a call from Hoskins, whom Elmore felt bound to visit the following morning on his way to the library, and inform of his belief that the enemy had quitted Venice, and that the whole affair was probably at an end. He was strengthened in this opinion by Mrs. Elmore's fear that she might have been colder than she supposed ; she hoped that she had not hurt the poor young fellow's feelings ; and now that he was gone, and safely out of the way, Elmore hoped so too.

On his return from the library, his wife met him with an air of mystery before which his heart sank. "Owen," she said, " Lily has a letter."

" Not bad news from home, Celia ! "

" No ; a letter which she wishes to show you. It has just come. As I don't wish to influence you, I would rather not be pre-

E

sent." Mrs. Elmore slipped out of the room, and Miss Mayhew glided gravely in, holding an open note in her hand, and looking into Elmore's eyes with a certain unfathomable candour, of which she had the secret.

"Here," she said, "is a letter which I think you ought to see at once, Professor Elmore;" and she gave him the note with an air of unconcern, which he afterward recalled without being able to determine whether it was real indifference or only the calm resulting from the transfer of the whole responsibility to him. She stood looking at him while he read :

MISS,

In this evening I am just arrived from Venise, 4 hours afterwards I have had the fortune to see you and to speake with you— and to favorite me of your gentil acquaint-anceship at rail-away. I never forgeet the moments I have seen you. Your pretty and nice figure had attached my heard so much, that I deserted in the hopiness to see you at Venise. And I was so lukely to speak with you cut too short, and in the possibility to understand all. I wished to go also in this Sonday to Venise, but I am sory that I cannot, beaucause I must feeled now the conse-quences of the deesrtation. Pray Miss to agree the assurance of my lov, and perhaps I will be so lukely to receive a notice from you Miss if I can hop a little (hapiness) sympathie. Très humble

E. VON EHRHARDT.

Elmore was not destitute of the national sense of humour; but he read this letter not only without amusement in its English, but with intense bitterness and renewed alarm. It appeared to him that the willingness of the ladies to put the affair in his hands had not strongly manifested itself till it had quite passed their own control, and had become a most embarrassing difficulty, —when, in fact, it was no longer a merit in them to confide it to him. In the resentment of that moment, his suspicions even accused his wife of desiring, from idle curiosity and sentiment, the accidental meeting which had resulted in this fresh aggression.

"Why did you show me this letter?" he asked harshly.

"Mrs. Elmore told me to do so," Lily answered.

"Did *you* wish me to see it?"

"I don't suppose I *wished* you to see it: I thought you ought to see it."

Elmore felt himself relenting a little.

"What do you want done about it?" he asked more gently.

"That is what I wished you to tell me," replied the girl.

"I can't tell you what you wish me to do, but I can tell you this, Miss Mayhew : this man's behaviour is totally irregular. He would not think of writing to an Italian or German girl in this way. If he desired to — to — pay attention to her, he would write to her father."

"Yes, that's what Mrs. Elmore said. She said she supposed he must think it was the American way."

"Mrs. Elmore," began her husband; but he arrested himself there, and said, " Very well. I want to know what I am to do. I want your full and explicit authority before I act. We will dismiss the fact of irregularity. We will suppose that it is fit and becoming for a gentleman who has twice met a young lady by accident,—or once by accident, and once by his own insistence—to write to her. Do you wish to continue the correspondence?"

" No."

Elmore looked into the eyes which dwelt full upon him, and, though they were clear as the windows of heaven, he hesitated. " I must do what you *say*, no matter what you mean, you know ?"

" I mean what I say."

" Perhaps," he suggested, " you would prefer to return him this letter with a few lines on your card."

" No. I should like him to know that I have shown it to you. I should think it a liberty for an American to write to me in that way after such a short acquaintance, and I don't see why I should tolerate it from a foreigner, though I suppose their customs *are* different."

" Then you wish me to write to him ?"

" Yes."

" And make an end of the matter once for all ?"

" Yes—"

" Very well, then." Elmore sat down at once, and wrote :—

Sir,—Miss Mayhew has handed me your note of yesterday, and begs me to express her very great surprise that you should have ventured to address her. She desires me also to add that you will consider at an end whatever acquaintance you suppose yourself to have formed with her.

Your obedient servant,
OWEN ELMORE.

He handed the note to Lily. "Yes, that will do," she said, in a low, steady voice. She drew a deep breath, and, laying the letter softly down, went out of the room into Mrs. Elmore's.

Elmore had not had time to kindle his sealing-wax when his wife appeared swiftly upon the scene.

"I want to see what you have written, Owen," she said.

"Don't talk to me, Celia," he replied, thrusting the wax into the candle-light. "You have put this affair entirely in my hands, and Lily approves of what I have written. I am sick of the thing, and I don't want any more talk about it."

"I *must* see it," said Mrs. Elmore, with finality, and possessed herself of the note. She ran it through, and then flung it on the table, and dropped into a chair, while the tears started to her eyes. "What a cold, cutting, merciless letter!" she cried.

"I hope he will think so," said Elmore, gathering it up from the table, and sealing it securely in its envelope.

"You're not going to *send* it!" exclaimed his wife.

" Yes, I am."

" I didn't suppose you could be so heartless."

" Very well, then, I *won't* send it," said
Elmore. " I put the affair in *your* hands.
What are you going to do about it ?"

" Nonsense ! "

" On the contrary, I 'm perfectly serious. I
don't see why you shouldn't manage the business. The gentleman is an acquaintance of
yours. *I* don't know him." Elmore rose and
put his hands in his pockets. " What do you
intend to do ? Do you like this clandestine
sort of thing to go on ? I dare say the fellow
only wishes to amuse himself by a flirtation
with a pretty American. But the question
is whether you wish him to do so. I 'm willing to lay his conduct to a misunderstanding
of our customs, and to suppose that he thinks
this is the way Americans do. I take the
matter at its best : he speaks to Lily on the
train without an introduction ; he joins you
in your walk without invitation ; he writes
to her without leave, and proposes to get up
a correspondence. It is all perfectly right
and proper, and will appear so to Lily's
friends when they hear of it. But I 'm curious to know how you 're going to manage the

sequel. Do you wish the affair to go on, and how long do you wish it to go on?"

"You know very well that I don't wish it to go on."

"Then you wish it broken off?"

"Of course I do."

"How?"

"I think there is such a thing as acting kindly and considerately. I don't see anything in Captain Ehrhardt's conduct that calls for *savage* treatment," said Mrs. Elmore.

"You would like to have him stopped, but stopped gradually. Well, I don't wish to be savage, either, and I will act upon any suggestion of yours. I want Lily's people to feel that we managed not only wisely but humanely in checking a man who was resolved to force his acquaintance upon her."

Mrs. Elmore thought a long while. Then she said: "Why, of course, Owen, you 're right about it. There *is* no other way. There couldn't be any kindness in checking him gradually. But I wish," she added sorrowfully, "that he had not been such a *complete* goose; and then we could have done something with him."

"I am obliged to him for the perfection which you regret, my dear. If he had been less complete, he would have been much harder to manage."

" Well," said Mrs. Elmore, rising, " I shall always say that he meant well. But send the letter."

Her husband did not wait for a second bidding. He carried it himself to the general post-office that there might be no mistake and no delay about it ; and a man who believed that he had a feeling and tender heart experienced a barbarous joy in the infliction of this pitiless snub. I do not say that it would not have been different if he had trusted at all in the sincerity of Captain Ehrhardt's passion ; but he was glad to discredit it. A misgiving to the other effect would have complicated the matter. But now he was perfectly free to disembarrass himself of a trouble which had so seriously threatened his peace. He was responsible to Miss Mayhew's family, and Mrs. Elmore herself could not say, then or afterward, that there was any other way open to him. I will not contend that his motives were wholly unselfish. No doubt a sense of personal annoyance, of offended decorum, of wounded respectability, qualified the zeal for Miss Mayhew's good which

prompted him.   He was still a young and in-
experienced man, confronted with a strange
perplexity : he did the best he could, and I
suppose it was the best that could be done.
At any rate, he had no regrets, and he went
cheerfully about the work of interesting Miss
Mayhew in the monuments and memories of
the city.

Since the decisive blow had been struck,
the ladies seemed to share his relief.   The
pursuit of Captain Ehrhardt, while it flattered, might well have alarmed, and the loss
of a not unpleasant excitement was made
good by a sense of perfect security.   Whatever repining Miss Mayhew indulged was
secret, or confided solely to Mrs. Elmore.
To Elmore himself she appeared in better
spirits than at first, or at least in a more
equable frame of mind.   To be sure, he did
not notice very particularly.   He took her
to the places and told her the things that
she ought to be interested in, and he con-
ceived a better opinion of her mind from the
quick intelligence with which she entered
into his own feelings in regard to them,
though he never could see any evidence of
the over-study for which she had been
taken from school.   He made her, like

Mrs. Elmore, the partner of his historical researches; he read his notes to both of them now; and when his wife was prevented from accompanying him, he went with Lily alone to visit the scenes of such events as his researches concerned, and to fill his mind with the local colour which he believed would give life and character to his studies of the past. They also went often to the theatre; and, though Lily could not understand the plays, she professed to be entertained, and she had a grateful appreciation of all his efforts in her behalf that amply repaid him. He grew fond of her society; he took a childish pleasure in having people in the streets turn and glance at the handsome girl by his side, of whose beauty and stylishness he became aware through the admiration looked over the shoulders of the Austrians, and openly spoken by the Italian populace. It did not occur to him that she might not enjoy the growth of their acquaintance in equal degree, that she fatigued herself with the appreciation of the memorable and the beautiful, and that she found these long rambles rather dull. He was a man of little conversation; and, unless Mrs. Elmore

was of the company, Miss Mayhew pursued
his pleasures for the most part in silence.
One evening, at the end of the week, his
wife asked, " Why do you always take Lily
through the Piazza on the side furthest from
where the officers sit ? Are you afraid of
her meeting Captain Ehrhardt ?"

" Oh, no ! I consider the Ehrhardt business settled. But you know the Italians
never walk on the officers' side."

" You are not an Italian. What do you
gain by flattering them up ? I should think
you might suppose a young girl had some
curiosity."

" I do ; and I do everything I can to
gratify her curiosity. I went to San Pietro
di Castello to-day, to show her where the
Brides of Venice were stolen."

" The oldest and dirtiest part of the city !
What *could* the child care for the Brides of
Venice ? Now be reasonable, Owen !"

" It 's a romantic story. I thought girls
liked such things,—about getting married."

" And that 's the reason you took her
yesterday to show her the Bucentaur that
the doges wedded the Adriatic in ! Well,
what was your idea in going with her to the
Cemetery of San Michele ?"

"I thought she would be interested. I had never been there before myself, and I thought it would be a good opportunity to verify a passage I was at work on. We always show people the cemetery at home."

"That was considerate. And why did you go to Canarregio on Wednesday?"

"I wished her to see the statue of Sior Antonio Rioba; you know it was the Venetian Pasquino in the Revolution of '48"—

"Charming!"

"And the Campo di Giustizia, where the executions used to take place."

"Delightful!"

"And—and—the house of Tintoretto," faltered Elmore.

"Delicious! She cares so much for Tintoretto! And you've been with her to the Jewish burying-ground at the Lido, and the Spanish synagogue in the Ghetto, and the fish-market at the Rialto, and you've shown her the house of Othello and the house of Desdemona, and the prisons in the ducal palace; and three nights you've taken us to the Piazza as soon as the Austrian band stopped playing, and all the interesting promenading was over, and those stuffy old Italians began to come to the caffès. Well,

I can tell you that's no way to amuse a
young girl. We must do something for her,
or she will die. She has come here from a
country where girls have always had the
best time in the world, and where the times
are livelier now than they ever were, with
all this excitement of the war going on ; and
here she is dropped down in the midst of
this absolute deadness : no calls, no pic-nics,
no parties, no dances—nothing ! We must
do something for her."

"Shall we give her a ball?" asked Elmore,
looking round the pretty little apartment.

"There's nothing going on among the
Italians. But you might get us invited to
the German Casino."

"I dare say. But I will not do that."

"Then we could go to the Luogotenenza,
to the receptions. Mr. Hoskins could call
with us, and they would send us cards."

"That would make us simply odious to
the Venetians, and our house would be
thronged with officers. What I've seen of
them doesn't make me particularly anxious
for the honour of their further acquaintance."

"Well, I don't ask you to do any of these
things," said Mrs. Elmore, who had, in

fact, mentioned them with the intention of insisting upon an abated claim. "But I think you *might* go and dine at one of the hotels — at the Danieli—instead of that Italian restaurant; and then Lily could see somebody at the table-d'hôte, and not simply *perish* of despair."

"I—I didn't suppose it was so bad as that," said Elmore.

"Why, of course, she hasn't said anything,—she's far too well-bred for that; but I can tell from my own feelings how she must suffer. I have you, Owen," she said tenderly, "but Lily has *nobody*. She has gone through this Ehrhardt business so well that I think we ought to do all we can to divert her mind."

"Well, now, Celia, you see the difficulty of our position,—the nature of the responsibility we have assumed. How are we possibly, here in Venice, to divert the mind of a young lady fresh from the parties and picnics of Patmos?"

"We can go and dine at the Danieli," replied Mrs. Elmore.

"Very well, let us go, then. But she will learn no Italian there. She will hear nothing but English from the travellers and

bad French from the waiters ; while at our
restaurant "—

" Pshaw !" cried Mrs. Elmore, "what
- does Lily care for Italian ?   I'm sure *I*
never want to hear another word of it."

At this desperate admission, Elmore quite
gave way ; he went to the Danieli the next
morning, and arranged to begin dining there
that day.   There is no denying that Miss
Mayhew showed an enthusiasm in prospect
of the change that even the sight of the
pillar to which Foscarini was hanged head
downwards for treason to the Republic had
not evoked.   She made herself look very
pretty, and she was visibly an impression at
the table-d'hôte when she sat down there.
Elmore had found places opposite an elderly
lady and quite a young gentleman, of English speech, but of not very English effect
otherwise, who bowed to Lily in acknowledgment of some former meeting.   The
old lady said, " So you've reached Venice
at last ?   I'm very pleased, for your sake,"
as if at some point of the progress thither
she had been privy to anxieties of Lily
about arriving at her destination ; and, in
fact, they had been in the same hotels at
Marseilles and Genoa.   The young gentle-

man said nothing, but he looked at Lily throughout the dinner, and seemed to take his eyes from her only when she glanced at him ; then he dropped his gaze to his neglected plate and blushed. When they left the table, he made haste to join the Elmores in the reading-room, where he contrived, with creditable skill, to get Lily apart from them for the examination of an illustrated newspaper, at which neither of them looked ; they remained chatting and laughing over it in entire irrelevancy till the elderly lady rose and said, "Herbert, Herbert ! I am ready to go now," upon which he did not seem at all so, but went submissively.

"Who are those people, Lily ?" asked Mrs. Elmore, as they walked towards Florian's for their after-dinner coffee. The Austrian band was playing in the centre of the Piazza, and the tall, blonde German officers promenaded back and forth with dark Hungarian women, who looked each like a princess of her race. The lights glittered upon them, and on the brilliant groups spread fan-wise out into the Piazza before' the caffès ; the scene seemed to shake and waver in the splendour, like something painted.

F

"Oh, their name is Andersen, or something like that; and they're from Helgoland, or some such place. I saw them first in Paris, but we didn't speak till we got to Marseilles. That's his aunt; they're English subjects, someway; and he's got an appointment in the civil service—I think he called it—in India, and he doesn't want to go; and I told him he ought to go to America. That's what I tell all these Europeans."

"It's the best advice for them," said Mrs. Elmore.

"They don't seem in any great haste to act upon it," laughed Miss Mayhew. "Who was the red-faced young man that seemed to know you, and stared so?"

"That's an English artist who is staying here. He has a curious name,—Rose-Black; and he is the most impudent and pushing man in the world. I wouldn't introduce him, because I saw he was just dying for it."

Miss Mayhew laughed, as she laughed at everything, not because she was amused, but because she was happy; this child-like gaiety of heart was great part of her charm.

Elmore had quieted his scruples as a good

Venetian by coming inside of the caffè while
the band played, instead of sitting outside
with the bad patriots ; but he put the ladies
next the window, and so they were not altogether sacrificed to his sympathy with the
dimostrazione.

VII.

THE next morning Elmore was called from
his bed—at no very early hour, it must
be owned, but at least before a nine o'clock
breakfast—to see a gentleman who was waiting in the parlour. He dressed hurriedly,
with a thousand exciting speculations in his
mind, and found Mr. Rose-Black looking
from the balcony window. "You have a
pleasant position here," he said easily, as he
turned about to meet Elmore's look of indignant demand. "I've come to ask all about
our friends the Andersens."

"I don't know anything about them," answered Elmore. "I never saw them before."

"Aöh!" said the painter. Elmore had
not invited him to sit down, but now he
dropped into a chair, with the air of asking
Elmore to explain himself. "The young
lady of your party seemed to know them.
How uncommonly pretty all your American
young girls are ! But I'm told they fade

very soon. I should like to make up a pic-
nic party with you all for the Lido."

"Thank you," replied Elmore stiffly.
"Miss Mayhew has seen the Lido."

"Aöh ! *That's* her name. It's a pretty
name." He looked through the open door
into the dining-room, where the table was
set for breakfast, with the usual water-
goblet at each plate. "I see you have beer
for breakfast. There's nothing so nice, you
know. Would you—would you mind giving me a glahs ?"

Through an undefined sense of the duties
of hospitality, Elmore was surprised by this
impudence into sending out to the next caffè
for a pitcher of beer. Rose-Black poured
himself out one glass and another till he
had emptied the pitcher, conversing affably
meanwhile with his silent host.

" *Why* didn't you turn him out of doors?"
demanded Mrs. Elmore, as soon as the
painter's departure allowed her to slip from
the closed door behind which she had been
imprisoned in her room.

"I did everything *but* that," replied her
husband, whom this interview had saddened
more than it had angered.

"You sent out for beer for him !"

" I didn't know but it might make him sick. Really, the thing is incredible. I think the man is cracked."

" He is an Englishman, and he thinks he can take any kind of liberty with us because we are Americans."

" That seems to be the prevalent impression among all the European nationalities," said Elmore. " Let's drop him for the present, and try to be more brutal in the future."

Mrs. Elmore, so far from dropping him, turned to Lily, who entered at that moment, and recounted the extraordinary adventure of the morning, which scarcely needed the embellishment of her fancy; it was not really a gallon of beer, but a quart, that Mr. Rose-Black had drunk. She enlarged upon previous aggressions of his, and said finally that they had to thank Mr. Ferris for his acquaintance.

" Ferris couldn't help himself," said Elmore. " He apologised to me afterward. The man got him into a corner. But he warned us about him as soon as he could. And Rose-Black would have made our acquaintance, any way. I believe he's crazy."

" I don't see how that helps the matter."

"It helps to explain it," concluded Elmore, with a sigh. " We can't refer everything to our being American lambs, and his being a ravening European wolf."

"Of course he came round to find out about Lily," said Mrs. Elmore. " The Andersens were a mere blind."

" Oh, Mrs. Elmore !" cried Lily in depre- cation.

The bell jangled. " That is the postman," said Mrs. Elmore.

There was a home-letter for Lily, and one from Lily's sister enclosed to Mrs. Elmore. The ladies rent them open, and lost them- selves in the cross-written pages ; and neither of them saw the dismay with which Elmore looked at the handwriting of the envelope addressed to him. His wife vaguely knew that he had a letter, and meant to ask him for it as soon as she should have finished her own. When she glanced at him again, he was staring at the smiling face of Miss May- hew, as she read her letter, with the wild regard of one who sees another in mortal peril, and can do nothing to avert the coming doom, but must dumbly await the catas- trophe.

"What is it, Owen?" asked his wife in a low voice.

He started from his trance, and struggled to answer quietly. "I've a letter here which I suppose I'd better show to you first."

They rose and went into the next room, Miss Mayhew following them with a bright, absent look, and then dropping her eyes again to her letter.

Elmore put the note he had received into his wife's hands without a word.

Sir,—My position permitted me to take a woman. I am a soldier, but I am an engineer—operateous, and I can exercise wherever my profession in the civil life. I have seen Miss Mayhew, and I have great sympathie for she. I think I will be lukely with her, if Miss Mayhew would be of the same intention of me.

If you believe, Sir, that my open and realy proposition will not offendere Miss Mayhew, pray to handed to her this note. Pray sir to excuse me the liberty to fatigue you, and to go over with silence if you would be of another intention.

Your obedient servant,
E. VON EHRHARDT.

Mrs. Elmore folded the letter carefully up and returned it to her husband. If he had perhaps dreaded some triumphant outburst from her, he ought to have been content with the thoroughly daunted look which she lifted to his, and the silence in which she suffered him to do justice to the writer.

"This is the letter of a gentleman, Celia," he said.

"Yes," she responded faintly.

"It puts another complexion on the affair entirely."

"Yes. Why did he wait a whole week?" she added.

"It is a serious matter with him. He had a right to take time for thinking it over." Elmore looked at the date of the Peschiera postmark, and then at that of Venice on the back of the envelope. "No, he wrote at once. This has been kept in the Venetian office, and probably read there by the authorities."

His wife did not heed the conjecture. "He began all wrong," she grieved. "Why couldn't he have behaved sensibly?"

"We must look at it from another point of view now," replied Elmore. "He has repaired his error by this letter."

"No, no ; he hasn't."

"The question is now what to do about

the changed situation.   This is an offer of
marriage.   It comes in the proper way.   It's
a very sincere and manly letter.   The man
has counted the whole cost : he's ready to
leave the army and go to America, if she
says so.   He's in love.   How can she refuse
him ?"

"Perhaps she isn't in love with him,"
said Mrs. Elmore.

"Oh !   That's true.   I hadn't thought of
that.   Then it's very simple."

"But I don't know that she isn't," murmured Mrs. Elmore.

"Well, ask her."

"How could *she* tell ?"

"How could she *tell ?*"

"Yes.   Do you suppose a child like that
can know her own mind in an instant ?"

"I should think she could."

"Well, she couldn't.   She liked the excitement,—the romanticality of it ; but she
doesn't know any more than you or I whether
she cares for him.   I don't suppose marriage
with anybody has ever seriously entered her
head yet."

"It will have to do so now," said Elmore
firmly.   "There's no help for it."

"I think the American plan is much

better," pouted Mrs. Elmore. "It's horrid to know that a man's in love with you, and wants to marry you, from the very start. Of course it makes you hate him."

"I dare say the American plan is better in this as in most other things. But we can't discuss abstractions, Celia. We must come down to business. What are we to do?"

"I don't know."

"We must submit the question to her."

"To that innocent, unsuspecting little thing? Never!" cried Mrs. Elmore.

"Then we must decide it, as he seems to expect we may, without reference to her," said her husband.

"No, that won't do. Let me think." Mrs. Elmore thought to so little purpose that she left the word to her husband again.

"You see we must lay the matter before her."

"Couldn't—couldn't we let him come to see us a while? Couldn't we explain our ways to him, and allow him to pay her attentions without letting her know about this letter?"

"I'm afraid he wouldn't understand,— that we couldn't make it clear to him," said Elmore. "If we invited him to the house he would consider it as an acceptance. He wants a categorical answer, and he has a right to it. It would be no kindness to a man with his ideas to take him on probation. He has behaved honourably, and we're bound to consider him."

"Oh, I don't think he's done anything so very great," said Mrs. Elmore, with that disposition we all have to disparage those who put us in difficulties.

"He's done everything he could do," said Elmore. "Shall I speak to Miss Mayhew?"

"No, you had better let me," sighed his wife. "I suppose we must. But I think it's horrid! Everything could have gone on so nicely if he hadn't been so impatient from the beginning. Of course she won't have him now. She will be scared, and that will be the end of it."

"I think you ought to be just to him, Celia. I can't help feeling for him. He has thrown himself upon our mercy, and he has a claim to right and thoughtful treatment."

"She won't have anything to do with him. You'll see."

"I shall be very glad of that," Elmore began.

"*Why* should you be glad of it?" demanded his wife.

He laughed. "I think I can safely leave his case in your hands. Don't go to the other extreme. If she married a German, he would let her black his boots,—like that general in Munich."

"Who is talking of marriage?" retorted Mrs. Elmore.

"Captain Ehrhardt and I. That's what it comes to; and it can't come to anything else. I like his courage in writing English, and it's wonderful how he hammers his meaning into it. 'Lukely' isn't bad, is it? And 'my position permitted me to take a woman'—I suppose he means that he has money enough to marry on—is delicious. Upon my word, I have a good deal of sympathie for he!"

"For shame, Owen! It's wicked to make fun of his English."

"My dear, I respect him for writing in English. The whole letter is touchingly brave and fine. Confound him! I wish I had never heard of him. What does he come bothering across my path for?"

"Oh, don't feel that way about it, Owen!" cried his wife. "It's cruel."

"I don't. I wish to treat him in the most generous manner; after all, it isn't his fault. But you must allow, Celia, that it's very annoying and extremely perplexing. We can't make up Miss Mayhew's mind for her. Even if we found out that she liked him, it would be only the beginning of our troubles. We've no right to give her away in marriage, or let her involve her affections here. But be judicious, Celia."

"It's easy enough to say that !"

"I'll be back in an hour," said Elmore. "I'm going to the square. We mustn't lose time."

As he passed out through the breakfast-room, Lily was sitting by the window with her letter in her lap, and a happy smile on her lips. When he came back she happened to be seated in the same place ; she still had a letter in her lap, but she was smiling no longer ; her face was turned from him as he entered, and he imagined a wistful droop in that corner of her mouth which showed on her profile.

But she rose very promptly, and with a heightened colour said, "I'm sorry to trouble you to answer another letter for me, Professor Elmore. I manage my correspondence at home myself, but here it seems to be different."

"It needn't be different here, Lily," said

Elmore kindly. "You can answer all the letters you receive in just the way you like. We don't doubt your discretion in the least. We will abide by any decision of yours, on any point that concerns yourself."

"Thank you," replied the girl; "but in this case I think you had better write." She kept slipping Ehrhardt's letter up and down between her thumb and finger against the palm of her left hand, and delayed giving it to him, as if she wished him to say something first.

"I suppose you and Celia have talked the matter over?"

"Yes."

"And I hope you have determined upon the course you are going to take, quite uninfluenced?"

"Oh, quite so."

"I feel bound to tell you," said Elmore, "that this gentleman has now done everything that we could expect of him, and has fully atoned for any error he committed in making your acquaintance."

"Yes, I understand that. Mrs. Elmore thought he might have written because he saw he had gone too far, and couldn't think of any other way out of it."

"That occurred to me, too, though I didn't

mention it. But we're bound to take the letter on its face, and that's open and honourable. Have you made up your mind?"

" Yes."

" Do you wish for delay? There is no reason for haste."

" There's no reason for delay, either," said the girl. Yet she did not give up the letter, or show any signs of intending to terminate the interview. " If I had had more experience, I should know how to act better; but I must do the best I can, without the experience. I think that even in a case like this we should try to do right, don't you?"

" Yes, above all other cases," said Elmore, with a laugh.

She flushed in recognition of her absurdity. " I mean that we oughtn't to let our feelings carry us away. I saw so many girls carried away by their feelings, when the first regiments went off, that I got a horror of it. I think it's wicked: it deceives both; and then you don't know how to break the engagement afterward."

" You're quite right, Lily," said Elmore, with a rising respect for the girl.

" Professor Elmore, can you believe that with all the attentions I've had, I've never seriously thought of getting married as the end of it all ?" she asked, looking him freely in the eyes.

"I can't understand it,—no man could, I suppose,—but I do believe it. Mrs. Elmore has often told me the same thing."

"And this—letter—it—means marriage."

"That and nothing else. The man who wrote it would consider himself cruelly wronged if you accepted his attentions without the distinct purpose of marrying him."

She drew a deep breath. "I shall have to ask you to write a refusal for me." But still she did not give him the letter.

"Have you made up your mind to that?"

"I can't make up my mind to anything else."

Elmore walked unhappily back and forth across the room. "I have seen something of international marriages since I've been in Europe," he said. "Sometimes they succeed ; but generally they're wretched failures. The barriers of different race, language, education, religion,—they're terrible barriers. It's very hard for a man and woman to understand each other at the best ; with these differences added, it's almost a hopeless case."

G

" Yes ; that 's what Mrs. Elmore said."

" And suppose you were married to an Austrian officer stationed in Italy. You would have *no* society outside of the garrison. Every other human creature that looked at you would hate you. And if you were ordered to some of those half barbaric principalities,—Moldavia or Wallachia, or into Hungary or Bohemia, — everywhere your husband would be an instrument for the suppression of an alien or disaffected population. What a fate for an American girl !"

" If he were good," said the girl, replying in the abstract, " she needn't care."

" If he were good, you needn't care. No. And he might leave the Austrian service, and go with you to America, as he hints. What could he do there? He might get an appointment in our army, though that 's not so easy now ; or he might go to Patmos, and live upon your friends till he found something to do in civil life."

Lily began a laugh. " Why, Professor Elmore, *I* don't want to marry him ! What in the world are you arguing with me for ?"

" Perhaps to convince myself. I feel that I oughtn't to let these considerations weigh as a feather in the balance if you are at all—

at all—ahem ! excuse me !—attached to him.
That, of course, outweighs everything else."

" But I 'm *not !*" cried the girl. " How
could I be ? I 've only met him twice. It
would be perfectly ridiculous. I *know* I 'm
not. I ought to know that if I know anything."

Years afterward it occurred to Elmore,
when he awoke one night, and his mind
without any reason flew back to this period
in Venice, that she might have been referring
the point to him for decision. But now it
only seemed to him that she was adding
force to her denial ; and he observed nothing
hysterical in the little laugh she gave.

" Well, then, we can't have it over too
soon. I 'll write now, if you will give me
his letter."

She put it behind her. " Professor
Elmore," she said, " I am not going to have
you think that he ever behaved in the least
presumingly. And whatever you think of
me, I must tell you that I suppose I talked
very freely with him,—just as freely, as I
should with an American. I didn't know
any better. He was very interesting, and I
was home-sick, and so glad to see any one
who could speak English. I suppose I was

a goose ; but I felt very far away from all my friends, and I was grateful for his kindness. Even if he had never written this last letter, I should always have said that he was a true gentleman."

"Well ?"

"That is all. I can't have him treated as if he were an adventurer."

"You want him dismissed ?"

"Yes."

"A man can't distinguish as to the terms of a dismissal. They 're always insolent,— more insolent than ever if you try to make them kindly. I should merely make this as short and sharp as possible."

"Yes," she said breathlessly, as if the idea affected her respiration.

"But I will show it to you, and I won't send it without your approval."

"Thank you. But I shall not want to see it. I 'd rather not." She was going out of the room.

"Will you leave me this letter ? You can have it again."

She turned red in giving it him. "I forgot. Why, it 's written to you, anyway !" she cried, with a laugh, and put the letter on the table.

The two doors opened and closed : one excluded Lily, and the other admitted Mrs. Elmore.

"Owen, I approve of all you said, except that about the form of the refusal. *I* will read what you say. I intend that it *shall* be made kindly."

"Very well. I'll copy a letter of yours, or write from your dictation."

"No ; you write it, and I'll criticise it."

"Oh, you talk as if I were eager to write the letter ! Can't you imagine it's being a very painful thing to me ?" he demanded.

"It didn't seem to be so before."

"Why, the situation wasn't the same before he wrote this letter !"

"I don't see how. He was as much in earnest then as he is now, and you had no pity for him."

"Oh, my goodness !" cried Elmore desperately. "Don't you see the difference ? He hadn't given any proof before"—

"Oh, proof, proof ! You men are always wanting proof ! What better proof could he have given than the way he followed her about ? Proof, indeed ! I suppose you'd like to have Lily prove that she doesn't care for him !"

"Yes," said Elmore sadly, "I should like very much to have her prove it."

"Well, you won't get her to. What makes you think she does?"

"I don't. Do you?"

"N-o," answered Mrs. Elmore reluctantly.

"Celia, Celia, you will drive me mad if you go on in this way! The girl has told me, over and over, that she wishes him dismissed. Why do you think she doesn't?"

"I don't. Who hinted such a thing? But I don't want you to *enjoy* doing it."

"*Enjoy* it? So you think I enjoy it! What do you suppose I'm made of? Perhaps you think I enjoyed catechising the child about her feelings toward him? Perhaps you think I enjoy the whole confounded affair? Well, I give it up. I will let it go. If I can't have your full and hearty support, I'll let it go. I'll do nothing about it."

He threw Ehrhardt's letter on the table, and went and sat down by the window. His wife took the letter up and read it over. "Why, you see he asks you to pass it over in silence if you don't consent."

"Does he?" asked Elmore. "I hadn't noticed that."

"Perhaps you'd better read some of your letters, Owen, before you answer them!"

"Really, I had forgotten. I had forgotten that the letter was written to me at all. I thought it was to Lily, and she had got to thinking so too. Well, then, I won't do anything about it." He drew a breath of relief.

"Perhaps," suggested his wife, "he asked that so as to leave himself some hope if he should happen to meet her again."

"And we don't wish him to have any hope."

Mrs. Elmore was silent.

"Celia," cried her husband indignantly, "I can't have you playing fast and loose with me in this matter!"

"I suppose I may have time to think?" she retorted.

"Yes, if you will tell me what you *do* think; but that I *must* know. It's a thing too vital in its consequences for me to act without your full concurrence. I won't take another step in it till I know just how far you have gone with me. If I may judge of what this man's influence upon Lily would be by the fact that he has brought us to the verge of the only real quarrel we've ever had" —

"Who's quarrelling, Owen?" asked Mrs. Elmore meekly. "I'm not."

"Well, well! we won't dispute about that. I want to know whether you thought with me that it was improper for him to address her in the car?"

"Yes."

"And still more improper for him to join you in the street?"

"Yes. But he was very gentlemanly."

"No matter about that. You were just as much annoyed as I was by his letter to her?"

"I don't know about annoyed. It scared me."

"Very well. And you approved of my answering it as I did?"

"I had nothing to do with it. I thought you were acting conscientiously. I'll say that much."

"You've got to say more. You have got to say you approved of it; for you know you did."

"Oh—*approved* of it? Yes!"

"That's all I want. Now I agree with you that if we pass this letter in silence, it will leave him with some hope. You agree with me that in a marriage between an

American girl and an Austrian officer the
chances would be ninety-nine to a hundred
against her happiness at the best."

" There are a great many unhappy marriages at home," said Mrs. Elmore impar-
tially.

" That isn't the point, Celia, and you know
it.   The point is whether you believe the
chances are for or against her in such a marriage.   Do you ?"

" Do I what ?"

" Agree with me ?"

" Yes ; but I say they *might* be *very* happy.
I shall always say that."

Elmore flung up his hands in despair.
" Well, then, say what shall be done now."

This was perhaps just what Mrs. Elmore
did not choose to say.   She was silent a
long time,—so long that Elmore said, "But
there's really no haste about it," and took
some notes of his history out of a drawer,
and began to look them over, with his back
turned to her.

" I never knew anything so heartless !"
she cried.   " Owen, this *must* be attended
to at once !   I can't have it hanging over
me any longer.   It will make me sick."

He turned abruptly round, and, seating

himself at the table, wrote a note, which he pushed across to her. It acknowledged the receipt of Captain von Ehrhardt's letter, and expressed Miss Mayhew's feeling that there was nothing in it to change her wish that the acquaintance should cease. In after years, the terms of this note did not always appear to Elmore wisely chosen or humanely considered ; but he stood at bay, and he struck mercilessly. In spite of the explicit concurrence of both Miss Mayhew and his wife, he felt as if they were throwing wholly upon him a responsibility whose fearfulness he did not then realise. Even in his wife's "Send it !" he was aware of a subtle reservation on her part.

VIII.

MRS. ELMORE and Lily again rose buoy-
antly from the conclusive event, but
he succumbed to it. For the delicate and
fastidious invalid, keeping his health evenly
from day to day upon the condition of a free
and peaceful mind, the strain had been too
much. He had a bad night, and the next
day a gastric trouble declared itself which
kept him in bed half the week, and left him
very weak and tremulous. His friends did
not forget him during this time. Hoskins
came regularly to see him, and supplied his
place at the table-d'hôte of the Danieli, going
to and fro with the ladies, and efficiently
protecting them from the depredations of
the Austrian soldiery. From Mr. Rose-Black
he could not protect them; and both the
ladies amused Elmore with a dramatisation
of how the Englishman had boldly outwitted
them, and trampled all their finessing under
foot, by simply walking up to them in the

reading-room, and saying, "This is Miss
Mayhew, I suppose," and putting himself at
once on the footing of an old family friend.
They read to Elmore, and they put his
papers in order, so that he did not know
where to find anything when he got well ;
but they always came home from the hotel
with some lively gossip, and this he liked.
They professed to recognise an anxiety on
the part of Mr. Andersen's aunt that his
mind should not be diverted from the civil
service in India by thoughts of young American ladies ; but she sent some delicacies to
Elmore, and one day she even came to call
with her nephew, in extreme reluctance and
anxiety as they pretended to him.

The next afternoon the young man called
alone, and Elmore, who was now on foot,
received him in the parlour, before the ladies
came in.   Mr. Andersen had a bunch of
flowers in one hand, and a small wooden box
containing a little turtle on a salad-leaf in
the other ; the poor animals are sold in the
Piazza at Venice for souvenirs of the city,
and people often carry them away.   Elmore
took the offerings simply, as he took everything in life, and interpreted them as an
expression, however odd, of Mr. Andersen's

sympathy with his recent sufferings, of which
he gave him some account ; but he practised
a decent self-denial here, and they were
already talking of the weather when the
ladies appeared. He hastened to exhibit
the tokens of Mr. Andersen's kind remembrance, and was mystified by the young
man's confusion, and the impatient, almost
contemptuous, air with which his wife listened to him.   Hoskins came in at that
moment to ask about Elmore's health, and
showed the hostile civility to Andersen
which young men use toward each other
in the presence of ladies ; and then, seeing
that the latter had secured the place at Miss
Mayhew's side on the sofa, he limped to the
easy chair near Mrs. Elmore, and fell into
talk with her about Rose-Black's pictures,
which he had just seen. They were based
upon an endeavour to trace the moral prin-
ciples believed by Mr. Ruskin to underlie
Venetian art, and they were very queer, so
Hoskins said ; he roughly sketched an idea
of some of them on a block he took from his
pocket.

Mr. Andersen and Lily went out upon one
of the high-railed balconies that overhung
the canal, and stood there, with their backs

to the others. She seemed to be listening, with averted face, while he, with his cheek leaning upon one hand and his elbow resting on the balcony rail, kept a pensive attitude after they had apparently ceased to speak. Something in their pose struck the sculptor's fancy, and he made a hasty sketch of them, and was showing it to the Elmores when Lily suddenly descended into the room again, and, saying something about its being quite dark, went out, and left Mr. Andersen to make his adieux to the others. He startled them by saying that he was to set off for India in the morning, and he went away very melancholy.

"Well, I don't know," said Hoskins, thoughtfully retouching his sketch, "that I should feel very lively about going out to India myself."

" He seems to be a very affectionate young fellow," observed Elmore, "and I've no doubt he will feel the separation from his friends. But I really don't know why he should have brought me a bouquet, and a small turtle in a box, on the eve of his departure."

"What ?" cried Hoskins, with a rude guffaw ; and when Elmore had showed his

gifts, Hoskins threw back his head and
laughed indecently. His behaviour nettled
Elmore, and it sent Mrs. Elmore prematurely
out of the room ; for, not content with his
explosions of laughter, he continued for some
time to amuse himself by touching up with
the point of his pencil the tail of the turtle
which he had turned out of its box upon
the table. At Mrs. Elmore's withdrawal he
stopped, and presently said good-night rather
soberly.

Then she returned. " Owen," she asked
sadly, " did you really think these flowers
and that turtle were for you ?"

" Why, yes," he answered.

" Well, I don't know whether I wouldn't
almost rather it had been a joke. I believe
that I would rather despise your heart than
your head. Why should Mr. Andersen
bring *you* flowers and a turtle ?"

" Upon my word, I don't know."

" They were for Lily ! And your mistake
has added another pang to the poor young
fellow's suffering. She has just refused him,"
she said ; and as Elmore continued to glare
blankly at her, she added : " She was refusing him there on the balcony while that
disgusting Mr. Hoskins was sketching them ;

and he had his hand up, that way, because he was crying."

"This is horrible, Celia !" cried Elmore. The scent of the flowers lying on the table seemed to choke him ; the turtle clawing about on the smooth surface looked demoniacal. "Why"——

"Now, don't ask me why she refused him, Owen. Of course she couldn't care for a boy like that. But he can't realise it, and it's just as miserable for him as if he were a thousand years old."

Elmore hung his head. "It was all a mistake. But how should I know any better? I am a straightforward man, Celia ; and I am unfit for the care that has been thrown upon me. It's more than I can bear. No, I'm *not* fit for it !" he cried at last ; and his wife, seeing him so crushed, now said something to console him.

"I know you're not. I see it more and more. But I know that you will do the best you can, and that you will always act from a good motive. Only *do* try to be more on your guard."

"I will—I will," he answered humbly.

He had a temptation, the next time he visited Hoskins, to tell him the awful secret, and to see how the situation of that night, with this lurid light upon it, affected him : it could do poor Andersen, now on his way to India, no harm. He yielded to his temptation, at the same time that he confessed his own blunder about the flowers.

Hoskins whistled. "I tell you what," he said, after a long pause, "there are some things in history that I never could realise, —like Mary, Queen of Scots, for instance, putting on her best things, and stepping down into the front parlour of that castle to have her head off. But a thing like this, happening on your own balcony, *helps* you to realise it."

"It helps you to realise it," assented Elmore, deeply oppressed by the tragic parallel.

"He's just beginning to feel it about now," said Hoskins, with strange *sang froid*. "I reckon it's a good deal like being shot. I didn't fully appreciate my little hit under a couple of days. Then I began to find out that something had happened. Look here," he added, "I want to show you something ;" and he pulled the wet cloth off a breadth of clay which he had set up on a board stayed against the wall. It was a bas-relief repre-

H

senting a female figure advancing from the left corner over a stretch of prairie towards a bulk of forest on the right ; bison, bear, and antelope fled before her ; a lifted hand shielded her eyes ; a star lit the fillet that bound her hair.

"That's the best thing you've done, Hoskins," said Elmore.   "What do you call it ?"

"Well, I haven't settled yet.   I *have* thought of 'Westward the Star of Empire,' but that's rather long ; and I've thought of 'American Enterprise.'   I ain't in any hurry to name it.   You like it, do you ?"

"I like it immensely !" cried Elmore. "You must let me bring the ladies to see it."

"Well, not just yet," said the sculptor, in some confusion.   "I want to get it a little further along first."

They stood looking together at the figure ; and when Elmore went away he puzzled himself about something in it,—he could not tell exactly what.   He thought he had seen that face and figure before, but this is what often occurs to the connoisseur of modern sculpture.   His mind heavily reverted to Lily and her suitors.   Take her in one way,

especially in her subordination to himself,
the girl was as simply a child as any in the
world, — good-hearted, tender, and sweet,
and, as he could see, without tendency to
flirtation. Take her in another way, con-
front her with a young and marriageable
man, and Elmore greatly feared that she
unconsciously set all her beauty and grace at
work to charm him ; another life seemed to
inform her, and irradiate from her, apart
from which she existed simple and childlike
still. In the security of his own deposited
affections, it appeared to him cruelly absurd
that a passion which any other pretty girl
might, and some other pretty girl in time
must, have kindled, should cling, when once
awakened, so inalienably to the pretty girl
who had, in a million chances, chanced to
awaken it. He wondered how much of this
constancy was natural, and how much merely
attributive and traditional, and whether human happiness or misery were increased by
it on the whole.

IX.

IN the respite which followed the dismissal
of Andersen, the English painter Rose-
Black visited the Elmores as often as the
servant, who had orders in his case to say
that they were *impediti*, failed of her duty.
They could not always escape him at the
caffè, and they would have left off dining at
the hotel but for the shame of feeling that he
had driven them away. If he had been an
Englishman repelling their advances, instead
of an Englishman pursuing them, he could
not have been more offensive. He affronted
their national as well as personal self-esteem;
he early declared himself a sympathiser with
the Southrons (as the London press then
called them), and he expressed the current
belief of his compatriots, that we were going
to the dogs.

"What do you really make of him, Owen?"
asked Mrs. Elmore, after an evening that, in
its improbable discomfort, had passed quite
like a nightmare.

" Well, I've been thinking a good deal
about him. I have been wondering if, in his
phenomenal way, he is not a final expression
of the national genius,—the stupid contempt
for the rights of others ; the tacit denial of
the rights of any people who are ac English
mercy ; the assumption that the courtesies
and decencies of life are for use exclusively
towards Englishmen."

This was in that embittered old war-time :
we have since learned how forbearing and
generous and amiable Englishmen are ; how
they never take advantage of any one they
believe stronger than themselves, or fail in
consideration for those they imagine their
superiors ; how you have but to show yourself successful in order to win their respect,
and even affection.

But for the present Mrs. Elmore replied to
her husband's perverted ideas, "Yes, it must
be so," and she supported him in the ineffec-
tual experiment of deferential politeness,
Christian charity, broad humanity, and savage rudeness upon Rose-Black. It was all
one to Rose-Black.

He took an air of serious protection towards Mrs. Elmore, and often gave her advice, while he practised an easy gallantry

with Lily, and ignored Elmore altogether.
His intimacy was superior to the accidents
of their moods, and their slights and snubs
were accepted apparently as interesting ex-
pressions of a civilisation about which he
was insatiably curious, especially as regarded the relations of young people. There
was no mistaking the fact that Rose-Black
in his way had fallen under the spell which
Elmore had learned to dread ; but there
was nothing to be done, and he helplessly
waited.   He saw what must come ; and one
evening it came, when Rose-Black, in more
than usually offensive patronage, lolled back
upon the sofa at Miss Mayhew's side, and
said, " About flirtations, now, in America,—
tell me something about flirtations. We've
heard so much about your American flirtations. We only have them with married
ladies, on the Continent, and I don't suppose
Mrs. Elmore would think of one."

"I don't know what you mean," said
Lily.   "I don't know anything about flirtations."

This seemed to amuse Rose-Black as an
uncommonly fine piece of American humour,
which was then just beginning to make its
way with the English. "Oh, but come,

now, you don't expect me to believe that,
you know. If you won't tell me, suppose
you show me what an American flirtation is
like. Suppose we get up a flirtation. How
should you begin?"

The girl rose with a more imposing air
than Elmore could have imagined of her
stature; but almost any woman can be
awful in emergencies. "I should begin by
bidding you good-evening," she answered,
and swept out of the room.

Elmore felt as if he had been left alone
with a man mortally hurt in combat, and
were likely to be arrested for the deed. He
gazed with fascination upon Rose-Black,
and wondered to see him stir, and at last
rise, and with some incoherent words to
them, get himself away. He dared not lift
his gaze to the man's eyes, lest he should
see there some reflection of the pain that
filled his own. He would have gone after
him, and tried to say something in con-
dolence, but he was quite helpless to move ;
and as he sat still, gazing at the door through
which Rose-Black disappeared, Mrs. Elmore
said quietly :—

" Well, really, I think that ought to be
the last of him. You see, she's quite able

to take care of herself when she knows her
ground.   You can't say that she has thrown
the brunt of this affair upon you, Owen."

"I am not so sure of that," sighed Elmore,
"I think I suffer less when I do it than
when I see it.   It's horrible."

"He deserved it, every bit," returned his
wife.

"Oh, I dare say," Elmore granted.   "But
the sight even of justice isn't pleasant, I
find."

"I don't understand you, Owen.   How
can you care so much for this impudent
wretch's little snub, and yet be so indifferent
about refusing Captain Ehrhardt?"

"I'm not indifferent about it, my dear.
I know that I did right, but I don't know
that I could do right under the same circumstances again."

In fact there were times when Elmore
found almost insupportable the absolute
conclusion to which that business had come.
It is hard to believe that anything has come
to an end in this world.   For a time, death
itself leaves the ache of an unsatisfied expectation, as if somehow the interrupted life
must go on, and there is no change we make
or suffer which is not denied by the sensa-

tion of daily habit.   If Ehrhardt had really
come back from the vague limbo to which
he had been so inexorably relegated, he
might only have restored the original situation in all its discomfort and apprehension ;
yet maintaining, as he did, this perfect
silence and absence, he established a hold
upon Elmore's imagination which deepened
because he could not discuss the matter
frankly with his wife.   He weakly feared
to let her know what was passing in his
thoughts, lest some misconception of hers
should turn them into self-accusal or urge
him to some attempt at the reparation towards which he wavered.   He really could
have done nothing that would not have
made the matter worse, and he confined
himself to speculating upon the character
and history of the man whom he knew only
by the incoherent hearsay of two excited
women, and by the brief record of hope and
passion left in the notes which Lily treasured
somewhere among the archives of a young
girl's triumphs.   He had a morbid curiosity
to see these letters again. but he dared not
ask for them ; and indeed it would have
been an idle self-indulgence : he remembered
them perfectly well.   Seeing Lily so in-

different, it was characteristic of him, in that safety from consequences which he chiefly loved, that he should tacitly constitute himself, in some sort, the champion of her rejected suitor, whose pain he luxuriously fancied in all its different stages and degrees. His indolent pity even developed into a sort of self-righteous abhorrence of the girl's hardness. But this was wholly within himself, and could work no sort of harm. If he never ventured to hint these feelings to his wife, he was still further from confessing them to Lily ; but once he approached the subject with Hoskins in a well-guarded generality relating to the different kinds of sensibility developed by the European and American civilisation. A recent suicide for love which excited all Venice at that time—an Austrian officer hopelessly attached to an Italian girl had shot himself—had suggested their talk, and given fresh poignancy to the misgivings in Elmore's mind.

"Well," said Hoskins, "those Dutch are queer. They don't look at women as respectfully as we do, and they mix up so much cabbage with their romance that you don't know exactly how to take them ; and yet here you find this fellow suffering just as much as a white man because the girl's folks won't let her have him.   In fact, I don't know but he suffered more than the average American citizen.   I think we have a great deal more common sense in our love-affairs.   We respect women more than any other people, and I think we show them more true politeness ; we let 'em have their way more, and get their finger into the pie right along, and it 's right we should : but we don't make fools of ourselves about them, as a general rule. We know they 're awfully nice, and they know we know it ; and it 's a perfectly understood thing all round.   We 've been used to each other all our lives, and they 're just as sensible as we are.   They like a fellow, when they do like him, about as well as any of 'em, but they know he 's a man and a brother after all, and he 's got ever so much human nature in him.   Well, now, I reckon one of these Dutch chaps, the first time he gets a chance to speak with a pretty girl, thinks he 's got hold of a goddess, and I suppose the girl feels just so about him.   Why, it 's natural they should—they 've never had any chance to know any better, and you 're feelings are apt to get the upper hand of you, at such times, any way. I don't blame 'em. One of 'em goes off and shoots himself, and the other one feels as if she was never going to get over it. Well, now, look at the way Miss Lily acted in that little business of hers : one of these girls over here would have had her head completely turned by that adventure ; but when she couldn't see her way exactly clear, she puts the case in your hands, and then stands by what you do, as calm as a clock."

"It was a very perplexing thing. I did the best I knew," said Elmore.

" Why, of course you did," cried Hoskins, "and she sees that as well as you or I do, and she stands by you accordingly. I tell you, that girl's got a cool head."

In his soul Elmore ungratefully and incousistently wished that her heart were not equally cool ; but he only said, "Yes, she is a good and sensible girl. I hope the—the— other one is equally resigned."

" Oh, he'll get along," answered Hoskins, with the indifference of one man for the sufferings of another in such matters. We are able to offer a brother very little comfort and scarcely any sympathy in those unhappy affairs of the heart which move women to a pretty compassion for a disappointed sister.

A man in love is in no wise interesting to us
for that reason ; and if he is unfortunate, we
hope at the furthest that he will have better
luck next time. It is only here and there
that a sentimentalist like Elmore stops to
pity him ; and it is not certain that even
he would have sighed over Captain Ehrhardt
if he had not been the means of his disappointment. As it was, he came away, feeling
that doubtless Ehrhardt had " got along,"
and resolved at least to spend no more un-
availing regrets upon him.

The time passed véry quietly now, and if
it had not been for Hoskins, the ladies must
have found it dull. He had nothing to do,
except as he made himself occupation with
his art, and he willingly bestowed on them
the leisure which Elmore could not find.
They went everywhere with him, and saw
the city to advantage through his efforts.
Doors, closed to ordinary curiosity, opened
to the magic of his card, and he showed a
pleasure in using such little privileges as his
position gave him, for their amusement. He
went upon errands for them ; he was like a
brother, with something more than a brother's
pliability ; he came half the time to breakfast
with them, and was always welcome to all.

He had the gift of extracting comfort from the darkest news about the war ; he was a prophet of unfailing good to the Union cause, and in many hours of despondency they willingly submitted to the authority of his greater experience, and took heart again.

"I like your indomitable hopefulness, Hoskins," said Elmore, on one of those occasions when the consul was turning defeat into victory. "There's a streak of unconscious poetry in it, just as there is in your taking up the subjects you do. I imagine that, so far as the judgment of the world goes, our fortunes are at the lowest ebb just now"—

"Oh, the world is wrong!" interrupted the consul. "Those London papers are all in the pay of the rebels."

"I mean that we have no sort of sympathy in Europe ; and yet here you are, embodying in your conception of 'Westward' the arrogant faith of the days when our destiny seemed universal union and universal dominion. There is something sublime to me in your treatment of such a work at such a time. I think an Italian, for instance, if his country were involved in a life and death struggle like this of ours, would have expressed something of the anxiety and apprehension of the time in it; but this conception of yours is as serenely undisturbed by the facts of the war as if secession had taken place in another planet. There is something Greek in that repose of feeling, triumphant over circumstance. It is like the calm beauty which makes you forget the anguish of the Laocoön."

"Is that so, Professor?" said Hoskins, blushing modestly, as an artist often must in these days of creative criticism. He seemed to reflect a while before he added, "Well, I reckon you're partly right. If we ever did go to smash, it would take us a whole generation to find it out. We have all been raised to put so much dependence on Uncle Sam, that if the old gentleman really did pass in his checks we should only think he was lying low for a new deal. never happened to think it out before, but I'm pretty sure it's so."

"Your work wouldn't be worth half so much to me if you had 'thought it out,'" said Elmore. "It's the unconsciousness of the faith that makes its chief value, as I said before; and there is another thing about it that interests and pleases me still more."

"What's that?" asked the sculptor.

"The instinctive way in which you have given the figure an entirely American quality. There was something very familiar to me in it, the first time you showed it, but I've only just been able to formulate my impression : I see now that while the spirit of your conception is Greek, you have given it, as you ought, the purest American expression. Your 'Westward' is no Hellenic goddess : she is a vivid and self-reliant American girl."

At these words, Hoskins reddened deeply, and seemed not to know where to look. Mrs. Elmore had the effect of escaping through the door into her own room, and Miss Mayhew ran out upon the balcony. Hoskins followed each in turn with a queer glance, and sat a moment in silence. Then he said, "Well, I reckon I must be going," and went rather abruptly, without offering to take leave of the ladies.

As soon as he was gone, Lily came in from the balcony, and whipped into Mrs. Elmore's room, from which she flashed again in swift retreat to her own, and was seen no more ; and then Mrs. Elmore came back, with a flushed face, to where her husband sat mystified.

"My dear," he said gravely, "I'm afraid you've hurt Mr. Hoskins's feelings."

"Do you think so?" she asked; and then she burst into a wild cry of laughter. "Oh, Owen, Owen! you will kill me yet!"

"Really," he replied with dignity, "I don't see any occasion in what I said for this extraordinary behaviour."

"Of course you don't, and that's just what makes the fun of it. So you found something familiar in Mr. Hoskins's statue from the first, did you?" she asked. "And you didn't notice anything particular in it?"

"Particular, particular?" he demanded, beginning to lose his patience at this.

"Oh," she exclaimed, "couldn't you see that it was Lily, all over again?"

Elmore laughed in turn. "Why, so it is; so it is! That accounts for everything that puzzled me. I don't wonder my maunderings amused you. It *was* ridiculous, to be sure! When in the world did she give him the sittings, and how did you manage to keep it from me so well?"

"Owen!" cried his wife, with terrible severity. "You don't think that Lily would *let* him put her into it?"

"Why, I supposed — I didn't know — I

I

don't see how he could have done it unless"—

" He did it without leave or licence," said
Mrs. Elmore. " We saw it all along, but he
never 'let on,' as he would say, about it, and
we never meant to say anything, of course."

" Then," replied Elmore, delighted with
the fact, "it has been a purely unconscious
piece of cerebration."

' Cerebration !" exclaimed Mrs. Elmore,
with more scorn than she knew how to express. " I should think as much !'

" Well, I don't know," said Elmore, with
the pique of a man who does not care to be
quite trampled under foot.   "I don't see
that the theory is so very unphilosophical."

"Oh, not at all!" mocked his wife. "It's
philosophical to the last degree. Be as philosophical as you please, Owen ; I shall love
you still the same." She came up to him
where he sat, and twisting her arm round
his face, patronisingly kissed him on top of
the head.   Then she released him, and left
him with another burst of derision.

X.

AFTER this Elmore had such an uncom-
fortable feeling that he hated to see
Hoskins again, and he was relieved when the
sculptor failed to make his usual call, the
next evening. He had not been at dinner
either, and he did not reappear for several
days. Then he merely said that he had been
spending the time at Chioggia, with a French
painter who was making some studies down
there, and they all took up the old routine
of their friendly life without embarrassment.

At first it seemed to Elmore that Lily was
a little shy of Hoskins, and he thought that
she resented his using her charm in his art ;
but before the evening wore away, he lost
this impression. They all got into a long talk
about home, and she took her place at the
piano and played some of the war-songs that
had begun to supersede the old negro melo-
dies. Then she wandered back to them,
with fingers that idly drifted over the keys,
and ended with "Stop dat knockin'," in

which Hoskins joined with his powerful bass
in the recitative "Let me in," and Elmore
himself had half a mind to attempt a part.
The sculptor rose as she struck the keys
with a final crash, but lingered, as his fashion
was when he had something to propose : if
he felt pretty sure that the thing would be
liked, he brought it in as if he had only happened to remember it. He now drew out a
large, square, ceremonious-looking envelope,
at which he glanced as if, after all, he was
rather surprised to see it, and said, "Oh, by-
the-by, Mrs. Elmore, I wish you 'd tell me
what to do about this thing. Here 's something that 's come to me in my official capa-
city, but it isn't exactly consular business,—
if it was, I don't believe I should ask *any*
lady for instructions,—and I don't know exactly what to do. It 's so long since I cor-
responded with a princess that I don't even
know how to answer her letter."

The ladies perhaps feared a hoax of some
sort, and would not ask to see the letter ;
and then Hoskins recognised his failure to
play upon their curiosity with a laugh, and
gave the letter to Mrs. Elmore. It was an
invitation to a mask ball, of which all Venice
had begun to speak. A great Russian lady,

who had come to spend the winter in the
Lagoons, and had taken a whole floor at one
of the hotels, had sent out her cards, apparently to all the available people in the city,
for the event which was to take place a fort-
night later. In the meantime, a thrill of pre-
paration was felt in various quarters, and the
ordinary course of life was interrupted in a
way that gave some idea of the old times,
when Venice was the capital of pleasure, and
everything yielded there to the great business of amusement. Mrs. Elmore had found
it impossible to get a pair of fine shoes
finished until after the ball ; a dress which
Lily had ordered could not be made ; their
laundress had given notice that for the present all fluting and quilling was out of the
question ; one already heard that the chief
Venetian perruquier and his assistants were
engaged for every moment of the forty-eight
hours before the ball, and that whoever had
him now must sit up with her hair dressed
for two nights at least. Mrs. Elmore had a
fanatical faith in these stories ; and while
agreeing with her husband, as a matter of
principle, that mask balls were wrong, and
that it was in bad taste for a foreigner to
insult the sorrow of Venice by a festivity of

the sort at such a time, she had secretly indulged longings which the sight of Hoskins's
invitation rendered almost insupportable.
Her longings were not for herself, but for
Lily : if she could provide Lily with the
experience of a masquerade in Venice, she
could overpay all the kindnesses that the
Mayhews had ever done her. It was an
ambition neither ignoble nor ungenerous,
and it was with a really heroic effort that
she silenced it in passing the invitation to
her husband, and simply saying to Hoskins,
"Of course you will go."

"I don't know about that," he answered.
"That's the point I want some advice on.
You see this document calls for a lady to fill
out the bill."

" Oh," returned Mrs. Elmore, "you will
find some Americans at the hotels.   You can
take them."

" Well, now, I was thinking, Mrs. Elmore,
that I should like to take you."

"Take   me !" she   echoed   tremulously.
" What an idea !   I 'm too old to go to mask
balls."

" You don't look it," suggested Hoskins.

"Oh, I couldn't go," she sighed.   "But
it 's very, very kind."

Hoskins dropped his head, and gave the low chuckle with which he confessed any little bit of humbug. " Well, you *or* Miss Lily."

Lily had retired to the other side of the room as soon as the parley about the invitation began. Without asking or seeing, she knew what was in the note, and now she felt it right to make a feint of not knowing what Mrs. Elmore meant when she asked, " What do *you* say, Lily ?"

When the question was duly explained to her, she answered languidly, "I don't know. Do you think I 'd better ?"

" I might as well make a clean breast of it, first as last," said Hoskins. " I thought perhaps Mrs. Elmore might refuse, she 's so stiff about some things,"—here he gave that chuckle of his,—" and so I came prepared for contingencies. It occurred to me that it mightn't be quite the thing, and so I went round to the Spanish consul and asked him how he thought it would do for me to matronise a young lady if I could get one, and he said he didn't think it would do at all." Hoskins let this adverse decision sink into the breasts of his listeners before he added : " But he said that he was going

with his wife, and that if we would come
along she could matronise us both. I don't
know how it would work," he concluded im-
partially.

They all looked at Elmore, who stood
holding the princess's missive in his hand,
and darkly forecasting the chances of consent and denial. At the first suggestion of
the matter, a reckless hope that this ball
might bring Ehrhardt above their horizon
again sprang up in his heart, and became a
desperate fear when the whole responsibility
of action was, as usual, left with him. He
stood, feeling that Hoskins had used him
very ill.

"I suppose," began Mrs. Elmore very
thoughtfully, "that this will be something
quite in the style of the old masquerades
under the Republic."

"Regular Ridotto business, the Spanish
consul says," answered Hoskins.

"It might be very useful to you, Owen,"
she resumed, "in an historical way, if Lily
were to go and take notes of everything ; so
that when you came to that period you could
describe its corruptions intelligently."

Elmore laughed. "I never thought of
that, my dear," he said, returning the in-

vitation to Hoskins. "Your historical sense
has been awakened late, but it promises to
be very active. Lily had better go, by all
means, and I shall depend upon her coming
home with very full notes upon her dance-
list."

They laughed at the professor's sarcasm,
and Hoskins, having undertaken to see that
the last claims of etiquette were satisfied by
getting an invitation sent to Miss Mayhew
through the Spanish consul, went off, and left
the ladies to the discussion of ways and means.
Mrs. Elmore said that of course it was now too
late to hope to get anything done, and then
set herself to devise the character that Lily
would have appeared in if there had been
time to get her ready, or if all the work-
people had not been so busy that it was
merely frantic to think of anything. She
first patriotically considered her as Columbia,
with the customary drapery of stars and
stripes and the cap of liberty. But while
holding that she would have looked very
pretty in the dress, Mrs. Elmore decided
that it would have been too hackneyed ; and
besides, everybody would have known instantly who it was.

"Why not have had her go in the character of Mr. Hoskins's 'Westward'?" suggested Elmore, with lazy irony.

" The very thing!" cried his wife. "Owen, you deserve great credit for thinking of that; no one else would have done it ! No one will dream what it means, and it will be great fun, letting them make it out. We must keep it a dead secret from Mr. Hoskins, and let her surprise him with it when he comes for her that evening. It will be a very pretty way of returning his compliment, and it will be a sort of delicate acknowledgment of his kindness in asking her, and in so many other ways. Yes, you've hit it exactly, Owen ; she shall go as 'Westward.'"

" Go?" echoed Elmore, who had with difficulty realised the rapid change of tense. "I thought you said you couldn't get her ready."

"We must manage somehow," replied Mrs. Elmore. And somehow a shoemaker for the sandals, a seamstress for the delicate flowing draperies, a hair-dresser for the adjustment of the young girl's rebellious abundance of hair beneath the star-lit fillet, were actually found,—with the help of Hoskins, as usual, though he was not suffered to know anything of the character to whose make-up he contributed. The perruquier, a personage of lordly address naturally, and of a dignity heightened by the demand in which he found himself, came early in the morning, and was received by Elmore with a self-possession that ill-comported with the solemnity of the occasion. "Sit down," said Elmore easily, pushing him a chair. "The ladies will be here presently."

"But I have no time to sit down, signore!" replied the artist, with an imperious bow, "and the ladies must be here instantly."

Mrs. Elmore always said that if she had not heard this conversation, and hurried in at once, the perruquier would have left them at that point. But she contrived to appease him by the manifestation of an intelligent sympathy; she made Lily leave her breakfast untasted, and submit her beautiful head to the touch of this man, with whom it was but a head of hair and nothing more; and in an hour the work was done. The artist whisked away the cloth which covered her shoulders, and crying, "Behold!" bowed splendidly to the spectators, and without waiting for criticism or suggestion, took his napoleon and went his way. All that day the work of his skill was sacredly guarded,

and the custodian of the treasure went about
with her head on her shoulders, as if it had
been temporarily placed in her keeping, and
were something she was not at all used to
taking care of. More than once Mrs. Elmore
had to warn her against sinister accidents.
"Remember, Lily," she said, "that if anything *did* happen, NOTHING could be done to
save you!" In spite of himself Elmore shared
these anxieties, and in the depths of his
wonted studies he found himself pursued and
harassed by vague apprehensions, which upon
analysis proved to be fears for Miss Lily's
hair. It was a great moment when the robe
came home—rather late—from the dress-
maker's, and was put on over Lily's head; but
from this thrilling rite Elmore was of course
excluded, and only knew of it afterwards by
hearsay. He did not see her till she came
out just before Hoskins arrived to fetch her
away, when she appeared radiantly perfect
in her dress, and in the air with which she
meant to carry it off. At Mrs. Elmore's direction she paraded dazzlingly up and down the
room a number of times, bending over to see
how her dress hung, as she walked. Mrs.
Elmore, with her head on one side, scruti-
nised her in every detail, and Elmore regarded

her young beauty and delight with a pride as innocent as her own. A dim regret, evaporating in a long sigh, which made the others laugh, recalled him to himself, as the bell rang and Hoskins appeared. He was received in a preconcerted silence, and he looked from one to the other with his queer, knowing smile, and took in the whole affair without a word.

"Isn't it a pretty idea?" said Mrs. Elmore. "Studied from an antique bas-relief, or just the same as an antique,—full of the anguish and the repose of the Laocoön."

"Mrs. Elmore," said the sculptor, "you 're too many for me. I reckon the procession had better start before I make a fool of myself. Well!" This was all Hoskins could say; but it sufficed. The ladies declared afterwards that if he had added a word more, it would have spoiled it. They had expected him to go to the ball in the character of a miner perhaps, or in that of a trapper of the great plains ; but he had chosen to appear more naturally as a courtier of the time of Louis XIV. "When you go in for a disguise," he explained, "you can't make it too complete ; and I consider that this limp of mine adds the last touch."

"It 's no use to sit up for them," Mrs.

Elmore said, when she and her husband had come in from calling good wishes and last instructions after them from the balcony, as their gondola pushed away.   "We shan't see anything more of *them* till morning. Now this," she added, "is something like the gaiety that people at home are always fancying in Europe.   Why, I can remember when I used to imagine that American tourists figured brilliantly in *salons* and *conversazioni*, and spent their time in masking and throwing *confetti* in carnival, and going to balls and opera.   I didn't know what American tourists were, then, and how dismally they moped about in hotels and galleries and churches.   And I didn't know how stupid Europe was socially,—how perfectly dead and buried it was, especially for young people.   It would be fun if things happened so that Lily never found it out!   I don't think two offers already,—or three, if you count Rose-Black, — are very bad for *any* girl ; and now this ball, coming right on top of it, where she will see hundreds of handsome officers !   Well, she 'll never miss Patmos, at this rate, will she ?"

"Perhaps she had better never have left Patmos," suggested Elmore gravely.

"I don't know what you mean, Owen," said his wife, as if hurt.

"I mean that it's a great pity she should give herself up to the same frivolous amusements here that she had there. The only good that Europe can do American girls who travel here is to keep them in total exile from what they call a good time,— from parties and attentions and flirtations; to force them, through the hard discipline of social deprivation, to take some interest in the things that make for civilisation,—in history, in art, in humanity."

"Now, there I differ with you, Owen. I think American girls are the nicest girls in the world, just as they are. And I don't see any harm in the things you think are so awful. You've lived so long here among your manuscripts that you've forgotten there is any such time as the present. If you are getting so Europeanised, I think the sooner we go home the better."

"*I* getting Europeanised!" began Elmore indignantly.

"Yes, Europeanised! And I don't want you to be so severe with Lily, Owen. The child stands in terror of you now; and if you keep on in this way, she can't draw a natural breath in the house."

There is always something flattering, at first, to a gentle and peaceable man in the notion of being terrible to any one ; Elmore melted at these words, and at the fear that he might have been, in some way that he could not think of, really harsh.

"I should be very sorry to distress her," he began.

"Well, you haven't distressed her yet," his wife relented. "Only you must be careful not to. She was going to be very circumspect, Owen, on your account, for she really appreciates the interest you take in her, and I think she sees that it won't do to be at all free with strangers over here. This ball will be a great education for Lily, —a *great* education. I 'm going to commence a letter to Sue about her costume, and all that, and leave it open to finish up when Lily gets home."

When she went to bed, she did not sleep till after the time when the girl ought to have come ; and when she awoke to a late breakfast, Lily had still not returned. By eleven o'clock she and Elmore had passed the stage of accusing themselves, and then

of accusing each other, for allowing Lily to
go in the way they had ; and had come to
the question of what they had better do,
and whether it was practicable to send to
the Spanish consulate and ask what had
become of her. They had resigned themselves to waiting for one half-hour longer,
when they heard her voice at the water-
gate, gaily forbidding Hoskins to come up ;
and running out upon the balcony, Mrs.
Elmore had a glimpse of the courtier, very
tawdry by daylight, re-entering his gondola,
and had only time to turn about when Lily
burst laughing into the room.

"Oh, don't look at me, Professor Elmore!"
she cried. " I 'm literally danced to rags ! "

Her dress and hair were splashed with
drippings from the wax candles ; she was
wildly decorated with favours from the
German, and one of these had been used
to pin up a rent which the spur of a hussar
had made in her robe ; her hair had escaped
from its fastenings during the night, and in
putting it back she had broken the star in
her fillet ; it was now kept in place by a bit
of black-and-yellow cord which an officer
had lent her. " He said he should claim it
of me the first time we met," she exclaimed

K

excitedly. "Why, Professor Elmore," she implored with a laugh, "don't look at me *so !*"

Grief and indignation were in his heart. "You look like the spectre of last night," he said with dreamy severity, and as if he saw her merely as a vision.

"Why, that's the way I *feel !*" she answered ; and with a reproachful "Owen !" his wife followed her flight to her room.

XI.

ELMORE went out for a long walk, from
which he returned disconsolate at dinner. He was one of those people, common
enough in our Puritan civilisation, who
would rather forego any pleasure than incur
the reaction which must follow with all the
keenness of remorse; and he always me-
chanically pitied (for the operation was not
a rational one) such unhappy persons as
he saw enjoying themselves. But he had
not meant to add bitterness to the anguish
which Lily would necessarily feel in retro-
spect of the night's gaiety; he had not
known that he was recognising, by those
unsparing words of his, the nervous misgivings in the girl's heart. He scarcely
dared ask, as he sat down at table with
Mrs. Elmore alone, whether Lily were
asleep.

"Asleep?" she echoed, in a low tone of
mystery. "I hope so."

"Celia, Celia!" he cried in despair.

"What shall I do? I feel terribly at what I said to her."

"Sh! At what you said to her? Oh yes! Yes, that was cruel. But there is so much else, poor child, that I had forgotten that."

He let his plate of soup stand untasted. "Why—why," he faltered, "didn't she enjoy herself?" And a historian of Venice, whose mind should have been wholly engaged in philosophising the republic's difficult past, hung abjectly upon the question whether a young girl had or had not had a good time at a ball.

"Yes. Oh, yes! She *enjoyed* herself— if that's all you require," replied his wife. "Of course she wouldn't have stayed so late if she hadn't enjoyed herself."

"No," he said in a tone which he tried to make leading; but his wife refused to be led by indirect methods. She ate her soup, but in a manner to carry increasing bitterness to Elmore with every spoonful.

"Come, Celia!" he cried at last, "tell me what has happened. You know how wretched this makes me. Tell me it, whatever it is. Of course, I must know it in the end. Are there any new complications?"

"No *new* complications," said his wife, as
if resenting the word. "But you make such
a bugbear of the least little matter that
there's no encouragement to tell you anything."

"Excuse me," he retorted, "I haven't
made a bugbear of this."

"You haven't had the opportunity." This
was so grossly unjust that Elmore merely
shrugged his shoulders and remained silent.
When it finally appeared that he was not
going to ask anything more, his wife added:
"If you could listen, like any one else, and
not interrupt with remarks that distort all
one's ideas"— Then, as he persisted in his
silence, she relented still further. "Why,
of course, as you say, you will have to know
it in the end. But I can tell you, to begin
with, Owen, that it's nothing you can do
anything about, or take hold of in any way.
Whatever it is, it's done and over; so it
needn't distress you at all."

"Ah, I've known some things done and
over that distressed me a great deal," he
suggested.

"The princess wasn't so very young, after
all," said Mrs. Elmore, as if this had been
the point in dispute, "but very fat and

jolly, and very kind. She wasn't in costume ; but there was a young countess with
her, helping receive, who appeared as Night,
—black tulle, you know, with silver stars.
The princess seemed to take a great fancy
to Lily,— the Russians always *have* sym-
pathised with us in the war,—and all the
time she wasn't dancing, the princess kept
her by her, holding her hand and patting
it. The officers—hundreds of them, in their
white uniforms and those magnificent hussar
dresses—were very obsequious to the princess, and Lily had only too many partners.
She says you can't imagine how splendid the
scene was, with all those different costumes,
and the rooms a perfect blaze of waxlights ;
the windows were battened, so that you
couldn't tell when it came daylight, and she
hadn't any idea how the time was passing.
They were not all in masks ; and there
didn't seem to be any regular hour for un-
masking. She can't tell just when the supper was, but she thinks it must have been
towards morning. She says Mr. Hoskins
got on capitally, and everybody seemed to
like him, he was so jolly and good-natured ;
and when they found out that he had been
wounded in the war, they made quite a belle

of him as he called it. The princess made a
point of introducing all the officers to Lily that
came up after they unmasked.   They paid
her the greatest attention, and you can easily
see that she was the prettiest girl there."

"I can believe that without seeing," said
Elmore, with magnanimous pride in the
loveliness that had made him so much
trouble.   "Well?"

"Well, they couldn't any of them get the
hang, as Mr. Hoskins said, of the character
she came in, for a good while; but when
they did, they thought it was the best idea
there : and it was all *your* idea, Owen," said
Mrs. Elmore, in accents of such tender pride
that he knew she must now be approaching
the difficult passage of her narration.   "It
was so perfectly new and unconventional.
She got on very well speaking Italian with
the officers, for she knew as much of it as
they did."

Here Mrs. Elmore paused, and glanced
hesitatingly at her husband.   "They only
made one little mistake; but that was at the
beginning, and they soon got over it."
Elmore suffered, but he did not ask what it
was, and his wife went on with smooth cau-
tion.   "Lily thought it was just as it is at

home, and she mustn't dance with any one
unless they had been introduced. So after
the first dance with the Spanish consul, as
her escort, a young officer came up and asked
her; and she refused, for she thought it was a
great piece of presumption. Afterwards the
princess told her she could dance with any
one, introduced or not, and so she did ; and
pretty soon she saw this first officer looking
at her very angrily, and going about speaking to others and glancing toward her. She
felt badly about it, when she saw how it was ;
and she got Mr. Hoskins to go and speak to
him. Mr. Hoskins asked him if he spoke
English, and the officer said No ; and it seems
that he didn't know Italian either, and Mr.
Hoskins tried him in Spanish,—he picked
up a little in New Mexico,—but the officer
didn't understand it; and all at once it occurred to Mr. Hoskins to say, 'Parlez-vous
Français?' and says the officer instantly,
'Oui, monsieur.'"

"Of course the man knew French. He
ought to have tried him with that in the
beginning. What did Hoskins say then?"
asked Elmore impatiently.

"He didn't say anything : that was all
the French he knew."

Elmore broke into a cry of laughter, and laughed on and on with the wild excess of a sad man when once he unpacks his heart in that way. His wife did not, perhaps, feel the absurdity as keenly as he, but she gladly laughed with him, for it smoothed her way to have him in this humour. " Mr. Hoskins just took him by the arm, and said, ' Here! you come along with me,' and led him up to the princess, where Lily was sitting ; and when the princess had explained to him, Lily rose, and mustered up enough French to say, ' Je vous prie, monsieur, de danser avec moi,' and after that they were the greatest friends."

" That was very pretty in her ; it was sovereignly gracious," said Elmore.

" Oh, if an American girl is left to manage for herself she can *always* manage !" cried Mrs. Elmore.

" Well, and what else ?" asked her husband.

" Oh, *I* don't know that it amounts to anything," said Mrs. Elmore ; but she did not delay further.

It appeared from what she went on to say that in the German,[1] which began not long

____

[1] *Anglice* Cotillion.

after midnight, there was a figure fancifully called the symphony, in which musical toys were distributed among the dancers in pairs ; the possessor of a small pandean pipe, or tin horn, went about sounding it, till he found some lady similarly equipped, when he demanded her in the dance.   In this way a tall mask, to whom a penny trumpet had fallen, was stalking to and fro among the waltzers, blowing the silly plaything with a disgusted air, when Lily, all unconscious of him, where she sat with her hand in that of her faithful princess, breathed a responsive note.   The mask was instantly at her side, and she was whirling away in the waltz. She tried to make him out, but she had already danced with so many people that she was unable to decide whether she had seen this mask before.   He was not disguised except by the little visor of black silk, coming down to the point of his nose ; his blonde whiskers escaped at either side, and his blonde moustache swept beneath, like the whiskers and moustaches of fifty other officers present, and he did not speak. This was a permissible caprice of his, but if she were resolved to make him speak, this also was a permissible caprice.   She made a whole turn of the room in studying up the Italian sentence with which she assailed him : "Perdoni, Maschera ; ma cosa ha detto ? Non ho ben inteso."

"Speak English, Mask," came the reply. "I did not say anything." It came certainly with a German accent, and with a foreigner's deliberation ; but it came at once, and clearly.

The English astonished her, and somehow it daunted her, for the mask spoke very gravely ; but she would not let him imagine that he had put her down, and she rejoined laughingly, "Oh, I knew that you hadn't spoken, but I thought I would make you."

"You think you can make one do what you will ?" asked the mask.

"Oh, no. I don't think I could make you tell me who you are, though I should like to make you."

"And why should you wish to know me ? If you met me in Piazza, you would not recognise my salutation."

"How do you know that ?" demanded Lily. "I don't know what you mean."

"Oh, it is understood yet already," answered the mask. "Your compatriot, with

whom you live, wishes to be well seen by
the Italians, and he would not let you bow
to an Austrian."

"That is not so," exclaimed Lily indignantly. "Professor Elmore wouldn't be so
mean ; and if he would, *I* shouldn't." She
was frightened, but she felt her spirit rising,
too. "You seem to know so well who I am :
do you think it is fair for you to keep me in
ignorance ?"

"I cannot remain masked without your
leave. Shall I unmask ? Do you insist ?"

"Oh, no," she replied. "You will have
to unmask at supper, and then I shall see
you. I'm not impatient. I prefer to keep
you for a mystery."

"You will be a mystery to me even when
you unmask," replied the mask gravely.

Lily was ill at ease, and she gave a little,
unsuccessful laugh. "You seem to take the
mystery very coolly," she said in default of
anything else.

"I have studied the American manner,"
replied the mask. "In America they take
everything coolly : life and death, love and
hate—all things."

"How do you know that? You have
never been in America."

"That is not necessary, if the Americans come here to show us."

"They are not true Americans, if they show you that," cried the girl.

"No?"

"But I see that you are only amusing yourself."

"And have you never amused yourself with me?"

"How could I," she demanded, "if I never saw you before?"

"But are you sure of that?" She did not answer, for in this masquerade banter she had somehow been growing unhappy. "Shall I prove to you that you have seen me before? You dare not let me unmask."

"Oh, I can wait till supper. I shall know then that I have never seen you before. I forbid you to unmask till supper! Will you obey?" she cried anxiously.

"I have obeyed in harder things," replied the mask.

She refused to recognise anything but meaningless badinage in his words. "Oh, as a soldier, yes!—you must be used to obeying orders." He did not reply, and she added, releasing her hand and slipping it into his arm, "I am tired now ; will you take me back to the princess ?"

He led her silently to her place, and left her with a profound bow.

"Now," said the princess, "they shall give you a little time to breathe. I will not let them make you dance every minute. They are indiscreet. You shall not take any of their musical instruments, and so you can fairly escape till supper."

"Thank you," said Lily absently, "that will be the best way ;" and she sat languidly watching the dancers. A young naval officer who spoke English ran across the floor to her.

"Come," he cried, "I shall have twenty duels on my hands if I let you rest here, when there are so many who wish to dance with you." He threw a pipe into her lap, and at the same moment a pipe sounded from the other side of the room.

"This is a conspiracy !" exclaimed the girl. "I will not have it ! I am not going to dance any more." She put the pipe back into his hands ; he placed it to his lips, and sounded it several times, and then dropped it into her lap again with a laugh, and vanished in the crowd.

"That little fellow is a rogue," said the

princess. "But he is not so bad as some of them. Monsieur," she cried in French to the fair-whiskered, tall mask who had already presented himself before Lily, "I will not permit it, if it is for a trick. You must unmask. I will dispense mademoiselle from dancing with you."

The mask did not reply, but turned his eyes upon Lily with an appeal which the holes of the visor seemed to intensify. "It is a promise," she said to the princess, rising in a sort of fascination. "I have forbidden him to unmask before supper."

"Oh, very well," answered the princess, "if that is the case. But make him bring you back soon : it is almost time."

"Did you hear, Mask?" asked the girl, as they waltzed away. "I will only make two turns of the room with you."

"Perdoni ?"

"This is too bad!" she exclaimed. "I will not be trifled with in this way. Either speak English, or unmask at once."

The mask again answered in Italian, with a repeated apology for not understanding. "You understand very well," retorted Lily, now really indignant, "and you know that this passes a jest."

"Can you speak German?" asked the mask in that tongue.

" Yes, a little, but I do not choose to speak it. If you have anything to say to me, you can say it in English."

" I cannot understand English," replied the mask, still in German, and now Lily thought the voice seemed changed ; but she clung to her belief that it was some hoax played at her expense, and she continued her efforts to make him answer her in English. The two turns round the room had stretched to half a dozen in this futile task, but she felt herself powerless to leave the mask, who for his part betrayed signs of embarrassment, as if he had undertaken a ruse of which he repented. A confused movement in the crowd and a sudden cessation of the music recalled her to herself, and she now took her partner's arm and hurried with him toward the place where she had left the princess. But the princess had already gone into the supper-room, and she had no other recourse than to follow with the stranger.

As they entered the supper-room she removed her little visor, and she felt, rather than saw, the mask put up his hand and lift away his own : he turned his head, and looked

down upon her with the face of a man she
had never seen before.

" Ah, you are there !" she heard the princess's voice calling to her from one of the
tables.   " How tired you look !   Here—here
I will make you drink this glass of wine."

The officer who brought her the wine gave
her his arm and led her to the princess, and
the late mask mixed with the two-score other
tall, blonde officers.

The night which stretched so far into the
day ended at last, and she followed Hoskins
down to their gondola.   He entered the boat
first, to give her his hand in stepping from the
riva; at the same moment she involuntarily
turned at the closing of the door behind her,
and found at her side the tall blonde mask,
or one of the masks, if there were two who
had danced with her.   He caught her hand
suddenly to his lips, and kissed it.

" Adieu — forgive !"   he   murmured   in
English, and then vanished in-doors again.

"Owen," said Mrs. Elmore dramatically at
the end of her narration, " who do you think
it could have been ?"

" I have no doubt as to who it was, Celia,"
replied Elmore, with a heat evidently quite

L

unexpected to his wife, "and if Lily has not been seriously annoyed by the matter, I am glad that it has happened. I have had my regrets—my doubts—whether I did not dismiss that man's pretensions too curtly, too unkindly. But I am convinced now that we did exactly right, and that she was wise never to bestow another thought upon him. A man capable of contriving a petty persecution of this sort—of pursuing a young girl who had rejected him in this shameless fashion,—is no gentleman."

"It *was* a persecution," said Mrs. Elmore with a dazed air, as if this view of the case had not occurred to her.

"A miserable, unworthy persecution!" repeated her husband.

"Yes."

"And we are well rid of him. He has relieved *me* by this last performance, immensely; and I trust that if Lily had any secret lingering regrets, he has given her a final lesson. Though I must say, in justice to her, poor girl, she didn't seem to need it."

Mrs. Elmore listened with a strange abeyance; she looked beaten and bewildered, while he vehemently uttered these words. She could not meet his eyes, with her consciousness of having her intended romance thrown back upon her hands ; and he seemed in nowise eager to meet hers, for whatever consciousness of his own.   "Well, it isn't certain that he was the one, after all," she said.

XII.

LONG after the ball Lily seemed to Elmore's eye not to have recovered her former tone. He thought she went about languidly, and that she was fitful and dreamy, breaking from moods of unwonted abstraction in bursts of gaiety as unnatural. She did not talk much of the ball; he could not be sure that she ever recurred to it of her own motion. Hoskins continued to come a great deal to the house, and she often talked with him for a whole evening; Elmore fancied she was very serious in these talks.

He wondered if Lily avoided him, or whether this was only an illusion of his; but in any case, he was glad that the girl seemed to find so much comfort in Hoskins's company, and when it occurred to him he always said something to encourage his visits. His wife was singularly quiescent at this time, as if, having accomplished all she wished in Lily's presence at the princess's ball, she was willing to rest for a while from further social endeavour. Life was falling into the dull routine again, and after the past shocks his nerves were gratefully clothing themselves in the old habits of tranquillity once more, when one day a letter came from the overseers of Patmos University, offering him the presidency of that institution on condition of his early return. The board had in view certain changes, intended to bring the university abreast with the times, which they hoped would meet his approval.

Among these was a modification of the name, which was hereafter to be Patmos University and Military Institute. The board not only believed that popular feeling demanded the introduction of military drill into the college, but they felt that a college which had been closed at the beginning of the Rebellion, through the dedication of its president and nearly all its students to the war, could in no way so gracefully recognise this proud fact of its history as by hereafter making war one of the arts which it taught. The board explained that of course Mr. Elmore would not be expected to take charge of this branch of instruction at once. A competent military assistant would be provided, and continued under him as long as he should deem his services essential. The letter closed with a cordial expression of the desire of Elmore's old friends to have him once more in their midst, at the close of labours which they were sure would do credit to the good old university and to the whole city of Patmos.

Elmore read this letter at breakfast, and silently handed it to his wife : they were alone, for Lily, as now often happened, had not yet risen. " Well ?" he said, when she had read it in her turn. She gave it back to him with a look in her dimmed eyes which he could not mistake. " I see there is no doubt of your feeling, Celia," he added.

" I don't wish to urge you," she replied, " but yes, I should like to go back. Yes, I am homesick. I have been afraid of it before, but this chance of returning makes it certain."

" And you see nothing ridiculous in my taking the presidency of a military institute ?"

" They say expressly that they don't expect you to give instruction in that branch."

" No, not immediately, it seems," he said, with his pensive irony. " And the history ?"

" Haven't you almost got notes enough ?"
Elmore laughed sadly. "I have been
here two years. It would take me twenty
years to write such a history of Venice as I
ought not to be ashamed to write ; it would
take me five years to scamp it as I thought
of doing. Oh, I dare say I had better go
back. I have neither the time nor the
money to give to a work I never was fit for,
—of whose magnitude even I was unable to
conceive."

"Don't say that !" cried his wife, with
the old sympathy. " You will write it yet,
I know you will. I would rather spend all
my days in this—watery mausoleum than
have you talk so, Owen !"

" Thank you, my dear ; but the work
won't be lost even if I give it up at this
point. I can do something with my material, I suppose. And you know that if I
didn't *wish* to give up my project I couldn't.
It 's a sign of my unfitness for it that I 'm
able to abandon it. The man who is born
to write the history of Venice will have no
volition in the matter ; he cannot leave it,
and he will not die till he has finished it."
He feebly crushed a bit of bread in his
fingers as he ended with this burst of feel-

ing, and he shook his head in sad negation
to his wife's tender protest,—" Oh, you will
come back some day to finish it !"

" No one ever comes back to finish a history of Venice," he said.

" Oh, yes, you will," she returned. "But
you need the rest from this kind of work,
now, just as you needed rest from your college work before.   You need a change of
standpoint,—and the American standpoint
will be the very thing for you."

" Perhaps so, perhaps so," he admitted.
" At any rate, this is a handsome offer, and
most kindly made, Celia.   It 's a great compliment.   I didn't suppose they valued me
so much."

" Of course they valued you, and they will
be very glad to get you.   I call it merely
letting the historic material ripen in your
mind, or else I shouldn't let you accept.
And I shall be glad to go home, Owen, on
Lily's account.   The child is getting no
good here : she 's drooping."

" Drooping ?"

" Yes.   Don't you see how she mopes
about ?"

" I 'm afraid—that—I have—noticed."

He was going to ask why she was droop-

ing ; but he could not. He said, recurring
to the letter of the overseers, "So Patmos
is a city."

"Of course it is by this time," said his
wife, "with all that prosperity !"

Now that they were determined to go,
their little preparations for return were soon
made ; and a week after Elmore had written
to accept the offer of the overseers, they were
ready to follow his letter home. Their decision was a blow to Hoskins under which he
visibly suffered ; and they did not realise till
then in what fond and affectionate friendship
he held them. He now frankly spent his
whole time with them ; he disconsolately
helped them pack, and he did all that a
consul can do to secure free entry for some
objects of Venice that they wished to get in
without payment of duties at New York.

He said a dozen times, "I don't know
what I *will* do when you're gone;" and
toward the last he alarmed them for his own
interests by beginning to say, "Well, I
don't see but what I will have to go along."

The last night but one Lily felt it her
duty to talk to him very seriously about his
future and what he owed to it. She told
him that he must stay in Italy till he could

bring home something that would honour
the great, precious, suffering country for
which he had fought so nobly, and which
they all loved. She made the tears come
into her eyes as she spoke, and when she
said that she should always be proud to be
associated with one of his works, Hoskins's
voice was quite husky in replying : "Is
that the way you feel about it ?" He went
away promising to remain at least till he
finished his bas-relief of Westward, and his
figure of the Pacific Slope ; and the next
morning he sent around by a *facchino* a note
to Lily.

She ran it through in the presence of the
Elmores, before whom she received it, and
then, with a cry of "I think Mr. Hoskins
is too *bad !*" she threw it into Mrs. Elmore's
lap, and, catching her handkerchief to her
eyes, she broke into tears and went out of
the room. The note read :—

DEAR MISS LILY,—Your kind interest in
me gives me courage to say something that
will very likely make me hateful to you
for evermore. But I have got to say it, and
you have got to know it ; and it's all the
worse for me if you have never suspected it.
I want to give my whole life to you, where-

ever and however you will have it. With
you by my side, I feel as if I could really
do something that you would not be ashamed
of in sculpture, and I believe that I could
make you happy. I suppose I believe this
because I love you very dearly, and I know
the chances are that you will not think this
is reason enough. But I would take one
chance in a million, and be only too glad of
it. I hope it will not worry you to read
this : as I said before, I had to tell you.
Perhaps it won't be altogether a surprise.
I might go on, but I suppose that until I
hear from you I had better give you as little
of my eloquence as possible.

CLAY HOSKINS.

"Well, upon my word," said Elmore, to
whom his wife had transferred the letter,
"this is very indelicate of Hoskins ! I must
say, I expected something better of him."
He looked at the note with a face of disgust.

"I don't know why you had a right to
expect anything better of him, as you call
it," retorted his wife. "It's perfectly
natural."

"Natural !" cried Elmore. "To put this
upon us at the last moment, when he knows
how much trouble I've"——

Lily re-entered the room as precipitately
as she had left it, and saved him from be-

traying himself as to the extent of his con-
fidences to Hoskins. "Professor Elmore,"
she said, bending her reddened eyes upon
him, "I want you to answer this letter for
me ; and I don't want you to write as you—
I mean, don't make it so cutting—so—so—
Why, I *like* Mr. Hoskins ! He's been so
kind ! And if you said anything to wound
his feelings"—

"I shall not do that, you may be sure ;
because, for one reason, I shall say nothing
at all to him," replied Elmore.

"You won't write to him ?" she gasped.

"No."

"Why, what shall I do-o-o-o ?" demanded
Lily, prolonging the syllable in a burst of
grief and astonishment.

"I don't know," answered Elmore.

"Owen," cried his wife, interfering for
the first time, in response to the look of
appeal that Lily turned upon her, "you
must write !

"Celia," he retorted boldly, "I *won't*
write. I have a genuine regard for Hoskins ;
I respect him, and I am very grateful to him
for all his kindness to you. He has been
like a brother to you both."

"Why, of course," interrupted Lily, "I

never thought of him as anything *but* a brother."

" And though I must say I think it would have been more thoughtful and—and—more considerate in him not to do this"—

" We did everything we could to fight him off from it," interrupted Mrs. Elmore, "both of us. We saw that it was coming, and we tried to stop it. But nothing would help. Perhaps, as he says, he *did* have to do it "

" I didn't dream of his—having any such —idea," said Elmore. " I felt so perfectly safe in his coming ; I trusted everything to him."

" I suppose you thought his wanting to come was all unconscious cerebration," said his wife disdainfully. " Well, now you see it wasn't."

" Yes ; but it's too late now to help it ; and though I think he ought to have spared us this, if he thought there was no hope for him, still I can't bring myself to inflict pain upon him, and the long and the short of it is, I *won't*."

" But how is he to be answered ?"

" I don't know. *You* can answer him."

" I could never do it in the world !"

" I own it 's difficult," said Elmore coldly.

" Oh, *I* will answer him—I will answer him," cried Lily, "rather than have any trouble about it. Here,—here," she said, reaching blindly for pen and paper, as she seated herself at Elmore's desk, "give me the ink, quick. Oh, dear ! What shall I say ? What date is it ?—the 25th ? And it doesn't matter about the day of the week. ' Dear Mr. Hoskins—Dear Mr. Hoskins— Dear Mr. Hosk '— Ought you to put Clay Hoskins, Esq., at the top or the bottom—or not at all, when you 've said Dear Mr. Hoskins ? Esquire seems so cold, anyway, and I *won't* put it ! ' Dear Mr. Hoskins '— Professor Elmore !" she implored reproach- fully, " tell me what to say !"

" That would be equivalent to writing the letter," he began.

" Well, write it, then," she said, throwing down the pen. " I don't *ask* you to dictate it. Write it, — write anything, — just in pencil, you know ; that won't commit you to anything ; they say a thing in pencil isn't legal,—and I 'll copy it out in the first per- son."

" Owen," said his wife, " you shall not refuse ! It 's inhuman, it 's inhospitable, when Lily wants you to, so ! Why, I never heard of such a thing !"

Elmore desperately caught up the sheet of paper on which Lily had written " Dear Mr. Hoskins," and groaning out " Well, well !" he added,—

I have your letter. Come to the station tomorrow and say good-bye to her whom you will yet live to thank for remaining only
Your friend,
ELIZABETH MAYHEW.

" There ! there, that will do beautifully— beautifully ! Oh, thank you, Professor Elmore, ever and ever so much ! That will save his feelings, and do everything," said Lily, sitting down again to copy it ; while Mrs. Elmore, looking over her shoulder, mingled her hysterical excitement with the girl's, and helped her out by sealing the note when it was finished and directed.

It accomplished at least one purpose intended. It kept Hoskins away till the final moment, and it brought him to the station for their adieux just before their train started. A consciousness of the absurdity of his part gave his face a humorously rueful cast. But he came pluckily to the mark. He marched straight up to the girl. "It's all right, Miss Lily," he said, and offered her his hand, which she had a strong impulse to cry over. Then he turned to Mrs. Elmore, and while he held her hand in his right, he placed his left affectionately on Elmore's shoulder, and, looking at Lily, he said, " You ought to get Miss Lily to help you out with your history, Professor ; she has a very good style,—quite a literary style, I should have said, if I hadn't known it was hers. I don't like her subjects, though." They broke into a forlorn laugh together ; he wrung their hands once more, without a word, and, without looking back, limped out of the waiting-room and out of their lives.

They did not know that this was really the last of Hoskins,—one never knows that any parting is the last,—and in their inability to conceive of a serious passion in him, they quickly consoled themselves for what he might suffer. They knew how kindly, how tenderly even, they felt towards him, and by that juggle with the emotions which we all practise at times, they found comfort for him in the fact. Another interest, another figure, began to occupy the morbid fancy of Elmore, and as they approached Peschiera his expectation became intense. There was no reason why it should exist; it would be by the thousandth chance, even if Ehrhardt were still there, that they should meet him at the railroad station, and there were a thousand chances that he was no longer in Peschiera. He could see that his wife and Lily were restive too; as the train drew into the station they nodded to each other, and pointed out of the window, as if to identify the spot where Lily had first noticed him; they laughed nervously, and it seemed to Elmore that he could not endure their laughter.

During that long wait which the train used to make in the old Austrian times at Peschiera, while the police authorities *viséd* the passports of those about to cross the frontier, Elmore continued perpetually alert. He was aware that he should not know Ehrhardt if he met him; but he should know that he was present from the looks of Lily and Mrs. Elmore, and he watched them. They dined well in waiting, while he impatiently trifled with the food, and ate next to nothing; and they calmly returned to their places in the train, to which he remounted after a last despairing glance

M

around the platform in a passion of disappointment.   The old longing not to be
left so wholly to the effect of what he had
done possessed him to the exclusion of all
other sensations, and as the train moved
away from the station he fell back against
the cushions of the carriage, sick that he
should never even have looked on the face
of the man in whose destiny he had played
so fatal a part.

XIII.

IN America, life soon settled into form about the daily duties of Elmore's place, and the daily pleasures and cares which his wife assumed as a leader in Patmos society. Their sojourn abroad conferred its distinction ; the day came when they regarded it as a brilliant episode, and it was only by fitful glimpses that they recognised its essential dulness. After they had been home a year or two, Elmore published his Story of Venice in the Lives of her Heroes, which fell into a ready oblivion ; he paid all the expenses of the book, and was puzzled that, in spite of this, the final settlement should still bring him in debt to his publishers. He did not understand, but he submitted ; and he accepted the failure of his book very meekly. If he could have chosen, he would have preferred that the *Saturday Review*, which alone noticed it in London with three lines of exquisite slight, should have passed

it in silence. But after all, he felt that the
book deserved no better fate. He always
spoke of it as unphilosophised and incom-
plete, without any just claim to being.

Lily had returned to her sister's household, but though she came home in the hey-
day of her young beauty, she failed somehow
to take up the story of her life just where
she had left it in Patmos. On the way
home she had refused an offer in London,
and shortly after her arrival in America she
received a letter from a young gentleman
whom she had casually seen in Geneva, and
who had found exile insupportable since
parting with her, and was ready to return
to his native land at her bidding ; but she
said nothing of these proposals till long afterwards to Professor Elmore, who, she said,
had suffered enough from her offers. She
went to all the parties and pic-nics, and had
abundant opportunities of flirtation and marriage ; but she neither flirted nor married.
She seemed to have greatly sobered ; and the
sound sense which she had always shown became more and more qualified with a thoughtful sweetness. At first, the relation between
her and the Elmores lost something of its intimacy ; but when, after several years, her

health gave way, a familiarity, even kinder than before, grew up. She used to like to come to them, and talk and laugh fondly over their old Venetian days. But often she sat pensive and absent, in the midst of these memories, and looked at Elmore with a regard which he found hard to bear: a gentle unconscious wonder it seemed, in which he imagined a shade of tender reproach.

When she recovered her health, after a journey to the West one winter, they saw that, by some subtle and indefinable difference, she was no longer a young girl. Perhaps it was because they had not met her for half a year. But perhaps it was age,—she was now thirty. However it was, Elmore recognised with a pang that the first youth at least had gone out of her voice and eyes. She only returned to arrange for a long sojourn in the West. She liked the climate and the people, she said ; and she seemed well and happy. She had planned starting a Kindergarten school in Omaha with another young lady ; she said that she wanted something to do. " She will end by marrying one of those Western widowers," said Mrs. Elmore.

" I wonder she didn't take poor old Hoskins," mused Elmore aloud.

"No, you don't, dear," said his wife, who had not grown less direct in dealing with him. "You know it would have been ridiculous; besides, she never cared anything for him,—she couldn't. You might as well wonder why she didn't take Captain Ehrhardt after you dismissed him."

"*I* dismissed him?"

"You wrote to him, didn't you?"

"Celia," cried Elmore, "this I *cannot* bear. Did I take a single step in that business without her request and your full approval? Didn't you both ask me to write?"

"Yes, I suppose we did."

"Suppose?"

"Well, we *did*,—if you want me to say it. And I'm not accusing you of anything. I know you acted for the best. But you can see yourself, can't you, that it was rather sudden to have it end so quickly"—

She did not finish her sentence, or he did not hear the close in the miserable absence into which he lapsed. "Celia," he asked at last, "do you think she—she had any feeling about him?"

"Oh," cried his wife restively, "how should *I* know?"

"I didn't suppose you *knew*," he pleaded. "I asked if you thought so."

"What would be the use of thinking anything about it? The matter can't be helped now. If you inferred from anything she said to you"—

"She told me repeatedly, in answer to questions as explicit as I could make them, that she wished him dismissed."

"Well, then, very likely she did."

"Very likely, Celia?"

"Yes. At any rate, it's too late now."

"Yes, it's too late now." He was silent again, and he began to walk the floor, after his old habit, without speaking. He was always mute when he was in pain, and he startled her with the anguish in which he now broke forth. "I give it up! I give it up! Celia, Celia, I'm afraid I did wrong! Yes, I'm afraid that I spoiled two lives. I ventured to lay my sacrilegious hands upon two hearts that a divine force was drawing together, and put them asunder. It was a lamentable blunder,—it was a crime!"

"Why, Owen, how strangely you talk! How could you have done any differently under the circumstances?"

"Oh, I could have done very differently.

I might have seen him, and talked with him brotherly, face to face. He was a fearless and generous soul! And I was meanly scared for my wretched little decorums, for my responsibility to her friends, and I gave him no chance."

"We wouldn't let you give him any," interrupted his wife.

"Don't try to deceive yourself, don't try to deceive *me*, Celia! I know well enough that you would have been glad to have me show mercy; and I would not even show him the poor grace of passing his offer in silence, if I must refuse it. I couldn't spare him even so much as that!"

"We decided—we both decided—that it would be better to cut off all hope at once," urged his wife.

"Ah, it was I who decided that—decided everything. Leave me to deal honestly with myself at last, Celia! I have tried long enough to believe that it was not I who did it!" The pent-up doubt of years, the long-silenced self-accusal, burst forth in his words. "Oh, I have suffered for it! I thought he must come back, somehow, as long as we stayed in Venice. When we left Peschiera without a glimpse of him—I wonder I outlived it.   But even if I had seen him there, what use would it have been?   Would I have tried to repair the wrong done?   What did I do but impute unmanly and impudent motives to him when he seized his chance to see her once more at that masquerade"—

"No, no, Owen!   He was not the one. Lily was satisfied of that long ago.   It was nothing but a chance, a coincidence.   Perhaps it was some one he had told about the affair"—

"No matter! no matter!   If I thought it was he, my blame is the same.   And she, poor girl,—in my lying compassion for him, I used to accuse her of cold-heartedness, of indifference!   I wonder she did not abhor the sight of me.   How has she ever tolerated the presence, the friendship, of a man who did her this irreparable wrong?   Yes, it has spoiled her life, and it was my work.   No, no, Celia! you and she had nothing to do with it, except as I forced your consent—it was my work; and, however I have tried openly and secretly to shirk it, I must bear this fearful responsibility."

He dropped into a chair, and hid his face in his hands, while his wife soothed him with loving excuses for what he had done.

with tender protests against the exaggera-
tions of his remorse.   She said that he had
done the only thing he could do ; that Lily
wished it, and that she never had blamed
him.   " Why, I don't believe she would
ever have married Captain Ehrhardt, any-
how.   She was full of that silly fancy of
hers about Dick Burton, all the time,—you
know how she used always to be talking
about him ; and when she came home and
found she had outgrown him, she had to
refuse him, and I suppose it 's that that 's
made her rather melancholy."   She explained
that Major Burton had become extremely
fat, that his moustache was too big and
black, and his laugh too loud ; there was
nothing left of him, in fact, but his empsy
sleeve, and Lily was too conscientious to
marry him merely for that.

   In fact, Elmore's regret did reflect a mon-
strous and distorted image of his conduct.
He had really acted the part of a prudent
and conscientious man ; he was perfectly
justifiable at every step ; but in the retro-
spect those steps which we can perfectly
justify sometimes seem to have cost so terribly that we look back even upon our sin-
ful stumblings with better heart.   Heaven

knows how such things will be at the last
day ; but at that moment there was no
wrong, no folly of his youth, of which Elmore did not think with more comfort than
of this passage in which he had been so wise
and right.

Of course the time came when he saw it
all differently again ; when his wife persuaded him that he had done the best that
any one could do with the responsibilities
that ought never to have been laid on a
man of his temperament and habits ; when
he even came to see that Lily's feeling was
a matter of pure conjecture with him, and
that so far as he knew she had never cared
anything for Ehrhardt. Yet he was glad to
have her away ; he did not like to talk of
her with his wife ; he did not think of her
if he could help it.

They heard from time to time through her
sister that her little enterprise in Omaha
was prospering, and that she was very con-
tented out West ; at last they heard directly
from her that she was going to be married.
Till then, Elmore had been dumbly tormented
in his sombre moods with the solution of a
problem at which his imagination vainly
toiled,—the problem of how some day she

and Ehrhardt should meet again and retrieve the error of the past for him. He contrived this encounter in a thousand different ways by a thousand different chances ; what he so passionately and sorrowfully longed for accomplished itself continually in his dreams, but only in his dreams.

In due course Lily married, and from all they could understand, very happily. Her husband was a clergyman, and she took particular interest in his parochial work, which her good heart and clear head especially qualified her to share with him. To connect her fate any longer with that of Ehrhardt was now not only absurd, it was improper ; yet Elmore sometimes found his fancy forgetfully at work as before. He could not at once realise that the tragedy of this romance, such as it was, remained to him alone, except perhaps as Ehrhardt shared it. With him, indeed, Elmore still sought to fret his remorse and keep it poignant, and his final failure to do so made him ashamed. But what lasting sorrow can one have from the disappointment of a man whom one has never seen ? If Lily could console herself, it seemed probable that Ehrhardt too had " got along."

TONELLI'S MARRIAGE.

TONELLI'S MARRIAGE.

THERE was no richer man in Venice than
Tommaso Tonelli, who had enough on
his florin a day; and none younger than he,
who owned himself forty-seven years old.
He led the cheerfullest life in the world, and
was quite a monster of content; but when
I come to sum up his pleasures, I fear that
I shall appear to my readers to be celebrating
a very insipid and monotonous existence. I
doubt if even a summary of his duties could
be made attractive to the conscientious imagination of hard-working people; for Tonelli's labours were not killing, nor, for that
matter, were those of any Venetian that I
ever knew. He had a stated employment
in the office of the notary Cenarotti; and he
passed there so much of every working day
as lies between nine and five o'clock, writing
upon deeds and conveyances and petitions

and other legal instruments for the notary,
who sat in an adjoining room, secluded from
nearly everything in this world but snuff.
He called Tonelli by the sound of a little
bell; and, when he turned to take a paper
from his safe, he seemed to be abstracting
some secret from long-lapsed centuries, which
he restored again, and locked back among
the dead ages when his clerk replaced the
document in his hands. These hands were
very soft and pale, and their owner was a
colourless old man, whose silvery hair fell
down a face nearly as white; but, as he has
almost nothing to do with the present affair,
I shall merely say that, having been com-
promised in the last revolution, he had been
obliged to live ever since in perfect retire-
ment, and that he seemed to have been
blanched in this social darkness as a plant
is blanched by growth in a cellar. His
enemies said that he was naturally a timid
man, but they could not deny that he had
seen things to make the brave afraid, or that
he had now every reason from the police to
be secret and cautious in his life. He could
hardly be called company for Tonelli, who
must have found the day intolerably long
but for the visit which the notary's pretty

granddaughter contrived to pay every morning in the cheerless *mezzà*. She commonly
appeared on some errand from her mother,
but her chief business seemed to be to share
with Tonelli the modest feast of rumour and
hearsay which he loved to furnish forth for
her, and from which doubtless she carried
back some fragments of gossip to the family
apartments. Tonelli called her, with that
mingled archness and tenderness of the
Venetians, his Paronsina; and, as he had
seen her grow up from the smallest possible
of Little Mistresses, there was no shyness
between them, and they were fully privi-
leged to each other's society by her mother.
When she flitted away again, Tonelli was
left to a stillness broken only by the soft
breathing of the old man in the next room,
and by the shrill discourse of his own loqua-
cious pen, so that he was commonly glad
enough when it came five o'clock. At this
hour he put on his black coat, that shone
with constant use, and his faithful silk hat,
worn down to the pasteboard with assiduous
brushing, and caught up a very jaunty cane
in his hand. Then, saluting the notary, he
took his way to the little restaurant, where
it was his custom to dine, and had his tripe

N

soup and his *risotto*, or dish of fried liver, in
the austere silence imposed by the presence
of a few poor Austrian captains and lieuten-
ants.   It was not that the Italians feared to
be overheard by these enemies ; but it was
good *dimostrazione* to be silent before the
oppressor, and not let him know that they
even enjoyed their dinners well enough,
under his government, to chat sociably over
them.   To tell the truth, this duty was an
irksome one to Tonelli, who liked far better
to dine, as he sometimes did, at a cook-shop,
where he met the folk of the people (*gente
del popolo*), as he called them ; and where,
though himself a person of civil condition,
he discoursed freely with the other guests,
and ate of their humble but relishing fare.
He was known among them as Sior Tommaso ; and they paid him a homage, which
they enjoyed equally with him, as a person
not only learned in the law, but a poet of
gift enough to write wedding and funeral
verses, and a veteran who had fought for
the dead Republic of Forty-eight.   They
honoured him as a most travelled gentleman, who had been in the Tyrol, and who
could have spoken German, if he had not
despised that tongue as the language of the

ugly Croats, like one born to it. Who, for example, spoke Venetian more elegantly than Sior Tommaso? or Tuscan, when he chose? and yet he was poor,—a man of that genius! Patience! When Garibaldi came, we should see! The *facchini* and gondoliers, who had been wagging their tongues all day at the church corners and ferries, were never tired of talking of this gifted friend of theirs, when having ended some impressive discourse or some dramatic story, he left them with a sudden adieu, and walked quickly away toward the Riva degli Schiavoni.

Here, whether he had dined at the cookshop, or at his more genteel and gloomy restaurant of the Bronze Horses, it was his custom to lounge an hour or two over a cup of coffee and a Virginia cigar at one of the many caffès, and to watch all the world as it passed to and fro on the quay. Tonelli was grey, he did not disown it; but he always maintained that his heart was still young, and that there was, moreover, a great difference in persons as to age, which told in his favour. So he loved to sit there, and look at the ladies; and he amused himself by inventing a pet name for every face he saw, which he used to teach to certain

friends of his, when they joined him over
his coffee. These friends were all young
enough to be his sons, and wise enough to
be his fathers; but they were always glad
to be with him, for he had so cheery a wit
and so good a heart that neither his years
nor his follies could make any one sad. His
kind face beamed with smiles, when Pennellini, chief among the youngsters in his
affections, appeared on the top of the nearest
bridge, and thence descended directly towards his little table. Then it was that he
drew out the straw which ran through the
centre of his long Virginia, and lighted the
pleasant weed, and gave himself up to the
delight of making aloud those comments on
the ladies which he had hitherto stifled in
his breast. Sometimes he would feign himself too deeply taken with a passing beauty
to remain quiet, and would make his friend
follow with him in chase of her to the Public
Gardens. But he was a fickle lover, and
wanted presently to get back to his caffè,
where, at decent intervals of days or weeks, he
would indulge himself in discovering a spy
in some harmless stranger, who, in going out,
looked curiously at the scar Tonelli's cheek had
brought from the battle of Vicenza in 1848.

"Something of a spy, no?" he asked at these times of the waiter, who, flattered by the penetration of a frequenter of his caffè, and the implication that it was thought seditious enough to be watched by the police, assumed a pensive importance, and answered, " Something of a spy, certainly."

Upon this Tonelli was commonly encouraged to proceed : " Did I ever tell you how I once sent one of those ugly muzzles out of a caffè? I knew him as soon as I saw him, —I am never mistaken in a spy,—and I went with my newspaper, and sat down close at his side. Then I whispered to him across the sheet, 'We are two.' 'Eh?' says he. ' It is a very small caffè, and there is no need of more than one,' and then I stared at him and frowned. He looks at me fixedly a moment, then gathers up his hat and gloves, and takes his pestilency off."

The waiter, who had heard this story, man and boy, a hundred times, made a quite successful show of enjoying it, as he walked away with Tonelli's fee of half a cent in his pocket. Tonelli then had left from his day's salary enough to pay for the ice which he ate at ten o'clock, but which he would sometimes forego, in order to give the money in charity,

though more commonly he indulged himself,
and put off the beggar with, "Another time,
my dear. I have no leisure now to discuss
those matters with thee."

On holidays this routine of Tonelli's life
was varied. In the forenoon he went to
mass at St. Mark's, to see the beauty and
fashion of the city ; and then he took a walk
with his four or five young friends, or went
with them to play at bowls, or even made
an excursion to the main-land where they
hired a carriage, and all those Venetians got
into it, like so many seamen, and drove the
horse with as little mercy as if he had been
a sail-boat. At seven o'clock Tonelli dined
with the notary, next whom he sat at table,
and for whom his quaint pleasantries had
a zest that inspired the Paronsina and her
mother to shout them into his dull ears, that
he might lose none of them. He laughed a
kind of faded laugh at them, and, rubbing
his pale hands together, showed by his act
that he did not think his best wine too good
for his kindly guest. The signora feigned
to take the same delight shown by her father
and daughter in Tonelli's drolleries ; but I
doubt if she had a great sense of his humour,
or, indeed, cared anything for it save as she

perceived that it gave pleasure to those she loved. Otherwise, however, she had a sincere regard for him, for he was most useful and devoted to her in her quality of widowed mother ; and if she could not feel wit, she could feel gratitude, which is perhaps the rarer gift, if not the more respectable.

The Little Mistress was dependent upon him for nearly all the pleasures and for the only excitements of her life. As a young girl she was at best a sort of caged bird, who had to be guarded against the youth of the other sex as if they, on their part, were so many marauding and ravening cats. During most days of the year the Paronsina's parrot had almost as much freedom as she. He could leave his gilded prison when he chose, and promenade the notary's house as far down as the marble well in the sunless court, and the Paronsina could do little more. The signora would as soon have thought of letting the parrot walk across their campo alone as her daughter, though the local dangers, either to bird or beauty, could not have been very great. The greengrocer of that sequestered campo was an old woman, the apothecary was grey, and his shop was haunted by none but superannuated physicians ; the baker, the butcher, the waiters at the caffè were all professionally, and, as purveyors to her family, out of the question ; the sacristan, who sometimes appeared at the perruquier's to get a coal from under the curling-tongs to kindle his censer, had but one eye, which he kept single to the service of the Church, and his perquisite of candle-drippings ; and I hazard little in saying that the Paronsina might have danced a polka around Campo San Giuseppe without jeopardy so far as concerned the handsome wood-carver, for his wife always sat in the shop beside him. Nevertheless a custom is not idly handed down by mother to daughter from the dawn of Christianity to the middle of the nineteenth century ; and I cannot deny that the local perruquier, though stricken in years, was still so far kept fresh by the immortal youth of the wax heads in his window as to have something beau-ish about him ; or that, just at the moment the Paronsina chanced to go into the campo alone, a *leone* from Florian's might not have been passing through it, when he would certainly have looked boldly at her, perhaps spoken to her, and possibly pounced at once upon her fluttering heart. So by day the Paronsina rarely went out, and she never emerged unattended from the silence and shadow of her grandfather's house.

If I were here telling a story of the Paronsina, or indeed any story at all, I might suffer myself to enlarge somewhat upon the daily order of her secluded life, and show how the seclusion of other Venetian girls was the widest liberty as compared with hers ; but I have no right to play with the reader's patience in a performance that can promise no excitement of incident, no charm of invention. Let him figure to himself, if he will, the ancient and half-ruined palace in which the notary dwelt, with a gallery running along one side of its inner court, the slender pillars supporting upon the corroded sculpture of their capitals a clinging vine, that dappled the floor with palpitant light and shadow in the afternoon sun. The gate, whose exquisite Saracenic arch grew into a carven flame, was surmounted by the armorial bearings of a family that died of its sins against the Serenest Republic long ago ; the marble cistern which stood in the middle of the court had still a ducal rose upon either of its four sides ; and little lions of stone perched upon the posts at the head of the marble stairway

climbing to the gallery, their fierce aspects
worn smooth and amiable by the contact of
hands that for many ages had mouldered in
tombs.   Toward the canal the palace windows had been immemorially bricked up for
some reason or caprice, and no morning sun-
light, save such as shone from the bright
eyes of the Paronsina, ever looked into the
dim halls.   It was a fit abode for such a man
as the notary, exiled in the heart of his
native city, and it was not unfriendly in its
influences to a quiet vegetation like the
signora's ; but to the Paronsina it was sad
as Venice itself, where, in some moods, I
have wondered that any sort of youth could
have the courage to exist.   Nevertheless,
the Paronsina had contrived to grow up
here a child of the gayest and archest spirit,
and to lead a life of due content, till after
her return home from the comparative freedom and society of Madame Prateux's school,
where she spent three years in learning all
polite accomplishments, and whence she
came, with brilliant hopes and romances
ready imagined, for any possible exigency
of the future.   She adored all the modern
Italian poets, and read their verse with that
stately and rhythmical fulness of voice which

often made it sublime and always pleasing.
She was a relentless patriot, an Italianissima
of the vividest green, white, and red ; and
she could interpret the historical novels of
her countrymen in their subtlest application
to the modern enemies of Italy. But all the
Paronsina's gifts and accomplishments were
to poor purpose, if they brought no young
men a-wooing under her balcony ; and it
was to no effect that her fervid fancy peopled
the palace's empty halls with stately and
gallant company out of Marco Visconti,
Nicolò de' Lapi, Margherita Pusterla, and
the other romances, since she could not hope
to receive any practicable offer of marriage
from the heroes thus assembled. Her grandfather invited no guests of more substantial
presence to his house. In fact, the police
watched him too narrowly to permit him to
receive society, even had he been so minded,
and for kindred reasons his family paid few
visits in the city. To leave Venice, except
for the autumnal *villeggiatura* was almost
out of the question ; repeated applications
at the Luogotenenza won the two ladies but
a tardy and scanty grace ; and the use of
the passport allowing them to spend a few
weeks in Florence was attended with so

much vexation, in coming and going upon
the imperial confines, and when they returned home they were subject to so great
fear of perquisition from the police, that it
was after all rather a mortification than a
pleasure that the government had given
them. The signora received her few acquaintances once a week ; but the Paronsina
found the old ladies tedious over their cups
of coffee or tumblers of lemonade, and declared that her mamma's reception days
were a martyrdom,—actually a martyrdom,
to her. She was full of life and the beautiful and tender longing of youth ; she had
a warm heart and a sprightly wit ; but
she led an existence scarce livelier than a
ghost's, and she was so poor in friends and
resources that she shuddered to think what
must become of her if Tonelli should die.
It was not possible, thanks to God ! that he
should marry.

The signora herself seldom cared to go
out, for the reason that it was too cold in
winter and too hot in summer. In the one
season she clung all day to her wadded arm-
chair, with her *scaldino* in her lap ; and in
the other season she found it a sufficient
diversion to sit in the great hall of the

palace, and be fanned by the salt breeze that came from the Adriatic through the vine-garlanded gallery. But besides this habitual inclemency of the weather, which forbade out-door exercise nearly the whole year, it was a displeasure to walk in Venice on account of the stairways of the bridges ; and the signora much preferred to wait till they went to the country in the autumn, when she always rode to take the air. The exceptions to her custom were formed by those after-dinner promenades which she sometimes made on holidays, in summer. Then she put on her richest black, and the Paronsina dressed herself in her best, and they both went to walk on the Molo, before the pillars of the lion and the saint, under the escort of Tonelli.

It often happened that, at the hour of their arrival on the Molo, the moon was coming up over the low bank of the Lido in the east, and all that prospect of ship-bordered quay, island, and lagoon, which, at its worst, is everything that heart can wish, was then at its best, and far beyond words to paint. On the right stretched the long Giudecca, with the domes and towers of its Palladian church, and the swelling

foliage of its gardens, and its line of ware-
houses—painted pink, as if even Business,
grateful to be tolerated amid such lovely
scenes, had striven to adorn herself. In
front lay San Giorgio, picturesque with its
church and pathetic with its political prisons ; and, further away to the east again,
the gloomy mass of the madhouse at San
Servolo, and then the slender campanili of
the Armenian convent rose over the gleam-
ing and tremulous water. Tonelli took in
the beauty of the scene with no more consciousness than a bird ; but the Paronsina
had learnt from her romantic poets and
novelists to be complimentary to prospects,
and her heart gurgled out in rapturous praises
of this. The unwonted freedom exhilarated
her ; there was intoxication in the encounter
of faces on the promenade, in the dazzle and
glimmer of the lights, and even in the music
of the Austrian band playing in the Piazza,
as it came purified to her patriotic ear by the
distance. There were none but Italians upon
the Molo, and one might walk there without
so much as touching an officer with the hem
of one's garment ; and, a little later, when
the band ceased playing, she should go with
the other Italians and possess the Piazza for

one blessed hour. In the meantime the Paronsina had a sharp little tongue ; and, after she had flattered the landscape, and had, from her true heart, once for all, saluted the promenaders as brothers and sisters in Italy, she did not mind making fun of their peculiarities of dress and person. She was signally sarcastic upon such ladies as Tonelli chanced to admire, and often so stung him with her jests that he was glad when Pennellini appeared, as he always did exactly at nine o'clock, and joined the ladies in their promenade, asking and answering all those questions of ceremony which form Venetian greeting. He was a youth of the most methodical exactness in his whole life, and could no more have arrived on the Molo a moment before or after nine than the bronze giants on the clock-tower could have hastened or lingered in striking the hour. Nature, which had made him thus punctual and precise, gave him also good looks, and a most amiable kindness of heart. The Paronsina cared nothing at all for him in his quality of handsome young fellow ; but she prized him as an acquaintance whom she might salute, and be saluted by, in a city where her grandfather's isolation kept her strange to nearly

all the faces she saw. Sometimes her evenings on the Molo wasted away without the
exchange of a word save with Tonelli, for her
mother seldom talked ; and then it was quite
possible her teasing was greater than his
patience, and that he grew taciturn under
her tongue. At such times she hailed Pennellini's appearance with a double delight ;
for, if he never joined in her attacks upon
Tonelli's favourites, he always enjoyed them,
and politely applauded them. If his friend
reproached him for this treason, he made him
every amend in answering, " She is jealous,
Tonelli,"—a wily compliment, which had the
most intense effect in coming from lips ordi-
narily so sincere as his.

The signora was weary of the promenade
long before the Austrian music ceased in the
Piazza, and was very glad when it came time
for them to leave the Molo, and go and sit
down to an ice at the Caffè Florian. This
was the supreme hour to the Paronsina, the
one heavenly excess of her restrained and
eventless life. All about her were scattered
tranquil Italian idlers, listening to the music
of the strolling minstrels who had succeeded
the military band ; on either hand sat her
friends, and she had thus the image of that

tender devotion without which a young girl is said not to be perfectly happy ; while the very heart of adventure seemed to bound in her exchange of glances with a handsome foreigner at a neighbouring table. On the other side of the Piazza a few officers still lingered at the Caffè Quadri ; and at the Specchi sundry groups of citizens in their dark dress contrasted well with these white uniforms ; but, for the most part, the moon and gas-jets shone upon the broad, empty space of the Piazza, whose loneliness the presence of a few belated promenaders only served to render conspicuous. As the giants hammered eleven upon the great bell, the Austrian sentinel, under the Ducal Palace, uttered a long, reverberating cry ; and soon after a patrol of soldiers clanked across the Piazza, and passed with echoing feet through the arcade into the narrow and devious streets beyond. The young girl found it hard to rend herself from the dreamy pleasure of the scene, or even to turn from the fine impersonal pain which the presence of the Austrians in the spectacle inflicted. All gave an impression something like that of the theatre, with the advantage that here one's self was part

of the pantomime ; and in those days, when
nearly everything but the puppet-shows was
forbidden to patriots, it was altogether the
greatest enjoyment possible to the Paronsina. The pensive charm of the place im-
bued all the little company so deeply that
they scarcely broke it, as they loitered slowly
homeward through the deserted Merceria.
When they reached the Campo San Salvatore,
on many a lovely summer's midnight, their
footsteps seemed to waken a nightingale
whose cage hung from a lofty balcony there ;
for suddenly, at their coming, the bird broke
into a wild and thrilling song, that touched
them all, and suffused the tender heart of
the Paronsina with an inexpressible pathos.

Alas ! she had so often returned thus from
the Piazza, and no stealthy footstep had followed hers homeward with love's persistence
and diffidence ! She was young, she knew,
and she thought not quite dull or hideous ;
but her spirit was as sole in that melancholy
city as if there were no youth but hers in
the world.   And a little later than this,
when she had her first affair, it did not origi-
nate in the Piazza, nor at all respond to her
expectations in a love-affair.   In fact, it was
altogether a business affair, and was managed

chiefly by Tonelli, who having met a young
doctor, laurelled the year before at Padua,
had heard him express so pungent a curiosity
to know what the Paronsina would have to
her dower, that he perceived he must be
madly in love with her. So with the consent of the signora he had arranged a correspondence between the young people ; and
all went on well at first,—the letters from
both passing through his hands. But his
office was anything but a sinecure, for while
the doctor was on his part of a cold temperament, and disposed to regard the affair
merely as a proper way of providing for
the natural affections, the Paronsina cared
nothing for him personally, and only viewed
him favourably as abstract matrimony,—as
the means of escaping from the bondage
of her girlhood and the sad seclusion of her
life into the world outside her grandfather's
house. So presently the correspondence fell
almost wholly upon Tonelli, who worked up
to the point of betrothal with an expense of
finesse and sentiment that would have made
his fortune in diplomacy or poetry. What
should he say now ? that stupid young Doctor
would cry in a desperation, when Tonelli
delicately reminded him that it was time to

answer the Paronsina's last note. Say this, that, and the other, Tonelli would answer, giving him the heads of a proper letter, which the Doctor took down on square bits of paper, neatly fashioned for writing prescriptions. "And for God's sake, caro dottore, put a little warmth into it!" The poor Doctor would try, but it must always end in Tonelli's suggesting and almost dictating every sentence; and then the letter, being carried to the Paronsina, made her laugh: "This is very pretty, my poor Tonelli, but it was never my onoratissimo dottore who thought of these tender compliments. Ah! that allusion to my mouth and eyes could only have come from the heart of a great poet. It is yours, Tonelli, don't deny it." And Tonelli, taken in his weak point of literature, could make but a feeble pretence of disclaiming the child of his fancy, while the Paronsina, being in this reckless humour, more than once responded to the Doctor in such fashion that in the end the inspiration of her altered and amended letter was Tonelli's. Even after the betrothal, the love-making languished, and the Doctor was indecently patient of the late day fixed for the marriage by the notary. In fact, the Doctor was very busy ; and, as his practice grew, the dower of the Paronsina dwindled in his fancy, till one day he treated the whole question of their marriage with such coldness and uncertainty in his talk with Tonelli, that the latter saw whither his thoughts were drifting, and went home with an indignant heart to the Paronsina, who joyfully sat down and wrote her first sincere letter to the Doctor, dismissing him.

"It is finished," she said, "and I am glad. After all, perhaps, I don't want to be any freer than I am ; and while I have you, Tonelli, I don't want a younger lover. Younger ? Diana ! You are in the flower of youth, and I believe you will never wither. Did that rogue of a Doctor, then, really give you the elixir of youth for writing him those letters ? Tell me, Tonelli, as a true friend, how long have you been forty-seven ? Ever since your fiftieth birthday ? Listen ! I have been more afraid of losing you than my sweetest Doctor. I thought you would be so much in love with love-making that you would go break-neck and court some one in earnest on your own account !"

Thus the Paronsina made a jest of the loss she had sustained ; but it was not pleasant to her, except as it dissolved a tie which love had done nothing to form. Her life seemed colder and vaguer after it, and the hour very far away when the handsome officers of her king (all good Venetians in those days called Victor Emanuel "our king") should come to drive out the Austrians and marry their victims. She scarcely enjoyed the prodigious privilege, offered her at this time in consideration of her bereavement, of going to the comedy, under Tonelli's protection and along with Pennellini and his sister, while the poor signora afterwards had real qualms of patriotism concerning the breach of public duty involved in this distraction of her daughter. She hoped that no one had recognised her at the theatre, otherwise they might have a warning from the Venetian Committee. "Thou knowest," she said to the Paronsina, "that they have even admonished the old Conte Tradonico, who loves the comedy better than his soul, and who used to go every evening. Thy aunt told me, and that the old rogue, when people ask him why he doesn't go to the play, answers, 'My mistress won't let me.' But fie! I am saying what young girls ought not to hear."

After the affair with the Doctor, I say,

life refused to return exactly to its old expression, and I suppose that, if what presently happened was ever to happen, it could not have occurred at a more appropriate time for a disaster, or at a time when its victims were less able to bear it. I do not know whether I have yet sufficiently indicated the fact, but the truth is, both the Paronsina and her mother had from long use come to regard Tonelli as a kind of property of theirs, which had no right in any way to alienate itself. They would have felt an attempt of this sort to be not only very absurd, but very wicked, in view of their affection for him and dependence upon him; and while the Paronsina thanked God that he would never marry, she had a deep conviction that he ought not to marry, even if he desired. It was at the same time perfectly natural, nay, filial, that she should herself be ready to desert this old friend, whom she felt so strictly bound to be faithful to her loneliness. As matters fell out, she had herself primarily to blame for Tonelli's loss; for, in that interval of disgust and ennui following the Doctor's dismissal, she had suffered him to seek his own pleasure on holiday evenings; and he had thus

wandered alone to the Piazza, and so, one
night, had seen a lady eating an ice there,
and fallen in love without more ado than
another man should drink a lemonade.

This facility came of habit, for Tonelli
had now been falling in love every other
day for some forty years ; and in that time
had broken the hearts of innumerable women
of all nations and classes.   The prettiest
water-carriers in his neighbourhood were in
love with him, as their mothers had been
before them, and ladies of noble condition
were believed to cherish passions for him.
Especially, gay and beautiful foreigners, as
they sat at Florian's, were taken with hopeless love of him ; and he could tell stories
of very romantic adventure in which he
figured as hero, though nearly always with
moral effect.   For example, there was the
countess from the mainland,—she merited
the sad distinction of being chief among
those who had vainly loved him, if you
could believe the poet who both inspired
and sang her passion.   When she took a
palace in Venice, he had been summoned
to her on the pretended business of a secretary ; but when she presented herself with
those idle accounts of her factor and tenants

on the mainland, her household expenses and her correspondence with her advocate, Tonelli perceived at once that it was upon a wholly different affair that she had desired to see him. She was a rich widow of forty, of a beauty supernaturally preserved and very great. "This is no place for thee, Tonelli mine," the secretary had said to himself, after a week had passed, and he had understood all the waywardness of that unhappy lady's intentions. "Thou art not too old, but thou art too wise, for these follies, though no saint;" and so had gathered up his personal effects, and secretly quitted the palace. But such was the countess's fury at his escape that she never paid him his week's salary; nor did she manifest the least gratitude that Tonelli, out of regard for her son, a very honest young man, refused in any way to identify her, but, to all except his closest friends, pretended that he had passed those terrible eight days on a visit to the country village where he was born. It showed Pennellini's ignorance of life that he should laugh at this history; and I prefer to treat it seriously, and to use it in explaining the precipitation with which Tonelli's latest inamorata returned his love.

Though, indeed, why should a lady of thirty, and from an obscure country town, hesitate to be enamoured of any eligible suitor who presented himself in Venice? It is not my duty to enter upon a detail or summary of Carlotta's character or condition, or to do more than indicate that, while she did not greatly excel in youth, good looks, or worldly gear, she had yet a little property, and was of that soft prettiness which is often more effective than downright beauty. There was, indeed, something very charming about her; and, if she was a blonde, I have no reason to think she was as fickle as the Venetian proverb paints that complexion of woman; or that she had not every quality which would have excused any one but Tonelli for thinking of marrying her.

After their first mute interview in the Piazza, the two lost no time in making each other's acquaintance; but though the affair was vigorously conducted, no one could say that it was not perfectly in order. Tonelli on the following day, which chanced to be Sunday, repaired to St. Mark's at the hour of the fashionable mass, where he gazed steadfastly at the lady during her

orisons, and whence, at a discreet distance,
he followed her home to the house of the
friends whom she was visiting. Somewhat
to his discomfiture at first, these proved to
be old acquaintances of his ; and when he
came at night to walk up and down under
their balconies, as bound in true love to do,
they made nothing of asking him in-doors,
and presenting him to his lady. But the
pair were not to be entirely balked of their
romance, and they still arranged stolen in-
terviews at church, where one furtively
whispered word had the value of whole
hours of unrestricted converse under the
roof of their friends. They quite refused to
take advantage of their anomalously easy
relations, beyond inquiry on his part as to
the amount of the lady's dower, and on hers
as to the permanence of Tonelli's employment. He in due form had Pennellini to
his confidant, and Carlotta unbosomed herself to her hostess ; and the affair was thus
conducted with such secrecy that not more
than two-thirds of Tonelli's acquaintance
knew anything about it when their engagement was announced.

There were now no circumstances to pre-
vent their early union, yet the happy con-

clusion was one to which Tonelli urged
himself after many secret and bitter displea-
sures of spirit. I am persuaded that his
love for Carlotta must have been most ardent
and sincere, for there was everything in his
history and reason against marriage. He
could not disown that he had hitherto led a
joyous and careless life, or that he was exactly fitted for the modest delights, the discreet variety, of his present state,—for his
daily routine at the notary's, his dinner at
the Bronze Horses or the cook-shop, his hour
at the caffè, his walks and excursions, for
his holiday banquet with the Cenarotti, and
his formal promenade with the ladies of that
family upon the Molo. He had a good employment, with a salary that held him above
want, and afforded him the small luxuries
already named ; and he had fixed habits of
work and of relaxation, which made both a
blessing. He had his chosen circle of intimate equals, who regarded him for his good-
heartedness and wit and foibles ; and his
little following of humble admirers, who
looked upon him as a gifted man in disgrace
with fortune. His friendships were as old
as they were secure and cordial ; he was
established in the kindliness of all who knew

him ; and he was flattered by the dependence of the Paronsina and her mother,
even when it was troublesome to him. He
had his past of sentiment and war, his present of story-telling and romance. He was
quite independent ; his sins, if he had any,
began and ended in himself, for none was
united to him so closely as to be hurt by
them ; and he was far too imprudent a man
to be taken for an example by any one. He
came and went as he listed, he did this or
that without question. With no heart chosen
yet from the world of woman's love, he was
still a young man, with hopes and affections
as pliable as a boy's. He had, in a word,
that reputation of good-fellow which in
Venice gives a man the title of *buon diavolo*,
but on which he does not anywhere turn his
back with impunity, either from his own
consciousness or from public opinion. There
never was such a thing in the world as both
good devil and good husband ; and even
with his betrothal Tonelli felt that his old,
careless, merry life of the hour ended, and
that he had tacitly recognised a future while
he was yet unable to cut the past. If one
has for twenty years made a jest of women,
however amiably and insincerely, one does

not propose to marry a woman without making a jest of one's self. The avenging remembrance of elderly people whose late matrimony had furnished food for Tonelli's wit now rose up to torment him, and in his morbid fancy the merriment he had caused was echoed back in his own derision.

It shocked him to find how quickly his secret took wing, and it annoyed him that all his acquaintances were so prompt to felicitate him. He imagined a latent mockery in their speeches, and he took them with an argumentative solemnity. He reasoned separately with his friends ; to all who spoke to him of his marriage he presented elaborate proofs that it was the wisest thing he could possibly do, and tried to give the affair a cold air of prudence. "You see, I am getting old ; that is to say, I am tired of this bachelor life in which I have no one to take care of me, if I fall sick, and to watch that the doctors do not put me to death. My pay is very little, but, with Carlotta's dower well invested, we shall both together live better than either of us lives alone. She is a careful woman, and will keep me neat and comfortable. She is not so young as some women I had thought to marry,—no, but so much

the better ; nobody will think her half so
charming as I do, and at my time of life
that is a great point gained. She is good,
and has an admirable disposition. She is
not spoiled by Venice, but as innocent as a
dove. O, I shall find myself very well with
her !"

This was the speech which with slight
modification Tonelli made over and over again
to all his friends but Pennellini. To him
he unmasked, and said boldly that at last
he was really in love ; and being gently
discouraged in what seemed his folly, and
incredulously laughed at, he grew angry, and
gave such proofs of his sincerity that Pennellini was convinced, and owned to himself,
" This madman is actually enamoured,—
enamoured like a cat ! Patience ! What will
ever those Cenarotti say ?"

In a little while poor Tonelli lost the
philosophic mind with which he had at first
received the congratulations of his friends,
and, from reasoning with them, fell to resenting their good wishes. Very little things
irritated him, and pleasantries which he had
taken in excellent part, time out of mind,
now raised his anger. His barber had for
many years been in the habit of saying, as he

applied the stick of fixature to Tonelli's
mustache, and gave it a jaunty upward curl,
" Now we will bestow that little dash of
youthfulness ; " and it both amazed and hurt
him to have Tonelli respond with a fierce
" Tsit ! " and say that this jest was proper in
its antiquity to the times of Romulus rather
than our own period, and so go out of the
shop without that "Adieu, old fellow,"
which he had never failed to give in twenty
years. "Capperi ! " said the barber, when
he emerged from a profound reverie into
which this outbreak had plunged him, and
in which he had remained holding the nose
of his next customer, and tweaking it to and
fro in the violence of his emotions, regardless
of those mumbled maledictions which the
lather would not permit the victim to articu-
late. "If Tonelli is so savage in his betrothal, we must wait for his marriage to
tame him. I am sorry. He was always
such a good devil."

But if many things annoyed Tonelli,
there were some that deeply wounded him,
and chiefly the fact that his betrothal seemed
to have fixed an impassable gulf of years
between him and all those young men whose
company he loved so well. He had really a

boy's heart, and he had consorted with them because he felt himself nearer their age than his own. Hitherto they had in no wise found his presence a restraint. They had always laughed, and told their loves, and spoken their young men's thoughts, and made their young men's jokes, without fear or shame, before the merry-hearted sage, who never offered good advice, if indeed he ever dreamed that there was a wiser philosophy than theirs. It had been as if he were the youngest among them ; but now, in spite of all that he or they could do, he seemed suddenly and irretrievably aged. They looked at him strangely, as if for the first time they saw that his moustache was grey, and his brow was not smooth like theirs, that there were crow's-feet at the corners of his kindly eyes. They could not phrase the vague feeling that haunted their hearts, or they would have said that Tonelli, in offering to marry, had voluntarily turned his back upon his youth ; that love, which would only have brought a richer bloom to their age, had breathed away for ever the autumnal blossom of his.

Something of this made itself felt in Tonelli's own consciousness, whenever he met

them, and he soon grew to avoid these com-
rades of his youth. It was therefore after a
purely accidental encounter with one of them,
and as he was passing into the Campo Sant'
Angelo, head down, and supporting himself
with an inexplicable sense of infirmity upon
the cane he was wont so jauntily to flourish,
that he heard himself addressed with, "I
say, master!" He looked up, and beheld
the fat madman who patrols that campo, and
who has the licence of his affliction to utter
insolences to whomsoever he will, leaning
against the door of a tobacconist's shop, with
his arms folded, and a lazy, mischievous smile
loitering down on his greasy face. As he
caught Tonelli's eye he nodded, " Eh ! I have
heard, master ;" while the idlers of that
neighbourhood, who relished and repeated
his incoherent pleasantries like the *mots* of
some great diner-out, gathered near with
expectant grins. Had Tonelli been altogether himself, as in other days, he would
have been far too wise to answer, " What
hast thou heard, poor animal ?"

" That you are going to take a mate when
most birds think of flying away," said the
madman. " Because it has been summer a
long time with you, master, you think it

will never be winter. Look out: the wolf doesn't eat the season."

The poor fool in these words seemed to utter a public voice of disapprobation and derision; and as the pitiless bystanders, who had many a time laughed with Tonelli, now laughed at him, joining in the applause which the madman himself led off, the miserable good devil walked away with a shiver, as if the weather had actually turned cold. It was not till he found himself in Carlotta's presence that the long summer appeared to return to him. Indeed, in her tenderness and his real love for her he won back all his youth again; and he found it of a truer and sweeter quality than he had known even when his years were few, while the gay old-bachelor life he had long led seemed to him a period of miserable loneliness and decrepitude. Mirrored in her fond eyes, he saw himself alert and handsome; and, since for the time being they were to each other all the world, we may be sure there was nothing in the world then to vex or shame Tonelli. The promises of the future, too, seemed not improbable of fulfilment, for they were not extravagant promises. These people's castle in the air was a house furnished from Carlotta's modest portion, and situated in a quarter of the city not too far from the Piazza, and convenient to a decent caffè, from which they could order a lemonade or a cup of coffee for visitors. Tonelli's stipend was to pay the housekeeping, as well as the minute wage of a servant-girl from the country ; and it was believed that they could save enough from that, and a little of Carlotta's money at interest, to go sometimes to the Malibran theatre or the Marionette, or even make an excursion to the mainland upon a holiday ; but if they could not, it was certainly better Italianism to stay at home ; and at least they could always walk to the Public Gardens. At one time, religious differences threatened to cloud this blissful vision of the future ; but it was finally agreed that Carlotta should go to mass and confession as often as she liked, and should not tease Tonelli about his soul ; while he, on his part, was not to speak ill of the pope except as a temporal prince, or of any of the priesthood except of the Jesuits when in company, in order to show that marriage had not made him a *codino*. For the like reason, no change was to be made in his custom of praising

Garibaldi and reviling the accursed Germans upon all safe occasions.

As Tonelli had nothing in the world but his salary and his slender wardrobe, Carlotta eagerly accepted the idea of a loss of family property during the Revolution. Of Tonelli's scar she was as proud as Tonelli himself.

When she came to speak of the acquaintance of all those young men, it seemed again like a breath from the north to her betrothed ; and he answered with a sigh, that this was an affair that had already finished itself. "I have long thought them too boyish for me," he said, "and I shall keep none of them but Pennellini, who is even older than I,—who, I believe, was never born, but created middle-aged out of the dust of the earth, like Adam. He is not a good devil, but he has every good quality."

While he thus praised his friend, Tonelli was meditating a service, which, when he asked it of Pennellini, had almost the effect to destroy their ancient amity. This was no less than the composition of those wedding-verses, without which, printed and exposed to view in all the shop-windows, no one in Venice feels himself adequately and truly married. Pennellini had never willingly

made a verse in his life ; and it was long before he understood Tonelli, when he urged
the delicate request. Then in vain he protested, recalcitrated. It was all an offence
to Tonelli's morbid soul, already irritated by
his friend's obtuseness, and eager to turn even
the reluctance of nature into insult. He took
his refusal for a sign that he, too, deserted
him ; and must be called back, after bidding
Pennellini adieu, to hear the only condition
on which the accursed sonnet would be furnished, namely, that it should not be signed
Pennellini, but an Affectionate Friend.
Never was sonnet cost poet so great anguish
as this : Pennellini went at it conscientiously
as if it were a problem in mathematics ; he
refreshed his prosody, he turned over Carrer,
he toiled a whole night, and in due time appeared as Tonelli's affectionate friend in all
the butchers' and bakers' windows. But it
had been too much to ask of him, and for a
while he felt the shock of Tonelli's unreason
and excess so much that there was a decided
coolness between them.

This important particular arranged, little
remained for Tonelli to do but to come to that
open understanding with the Paronsina and
her mother which he had long dreaded and

avoided.   He could not conceal from himself
that his marriage was a kind of desertion of
the two dear friends so dependent upon his
singleness, and he considered the case of the
Paronsina with a real remorse.   If his medi-
tated act sometimes appeared to him a gross
inconsistency and a satire upon all his former
life, he had still consoled himself with the
truth of his passion, and had found love its
own apology and comfort; but in its relation
to these lonely women, his love itself had no
fairer aspect than that of treason, and he
shrank from owning it before them with a
sense of guilt.   Some wild dreams of recon-
ciling his future with his past occasionally
haunted him ; but in his saner moments, he
perceived their folly.   Carlotta, he knew,
was good and patient, but she was nevertheless a woman, and she would never consent
that he should be to the Cenarotti all that
he had been ; these ladies also were very
kind and reasonable, but they too were
women, and incapable of accepting a less
perfect devotion.   Indeed, was not his proposed marriage too much like taking her
only son from the signora and giving the
Paronsina a stepmother ?   It was worse, and
so the ladies of the notary's family viewed

it, cherishing a resentment that grew with
Tonelli's delay to deal frankly with them ;
while Carlotta, on her part, was wounded
that these old friends should ignore his future wife so utterly.   On both sides evil was
stored up.

When Tonelli would still make a show of
fidelity to the Paronsina and her mother,
they accepted his awkward advances, the
latter with a cold visage, the former with a
sarcastic face and tongue.   He had managed
particularly ill with the Paronsina, who, having no romance of her own, would possibly
have come to enjoy the autumnal poetry of
his love if he had permitted.   But when she
first approached him on the subject of those
rumours she had heard, and treated them
with a natural derision, as involving the
most absurd and preposterous ideas, he, instead of suffering her jests, and then turning
her interest to his favour, resented them, and
closed his heart and its secret against her.
What could she do, thereafter, but feign
to avoid the subject, and adroitly touch it
with constant, invisible stings?   Alas ! it
did not need that she should ever speak to
Tonelli with the wicked intent she did ; at
this time he would have taken ill whatever

most innocent thing she said. When friends are to be estranged, they do not require a cause. They have but to doubt one another, and no forced forbearance or kindness between them can do aught but confirm their alienation. This is on the whole fortunate, for in this manner neither feels to blame for the broken friendship, and each can declare with perfect truth that he did all he could to maintain it. Tonelli said to himself, " If the Paronsina had treated the affair properly at first !" and the Paronsina thought, " If he had told me frankly about it to begin with !" Both had a latent heartache over their trouble, and both a sense of loss the more bitter because it was of loss still unacknowledged.

As the day fixed for Tonelli's wedding drew near, the rumour of it came to the Cenarotti from all their acquaintance. But when people spoke to them of it, as of something they must be fully and particularly informed of, the signora answered coldly, " It seems that we have not merited Tonelli's confidence ;" and the Paronsina received the gossip with an air of clearly affected surprise, and a " *Davvero !*" that at least discomfited the tale-bearers.

The consciousness of the unworthy part he was acting toward these ladies had come at last to poison the pleasure of Tonelli's wooing, even in Carlotta's presence ; yet I suppose he would still have let his wedding-day come and go, and been married beyond hope of atonement, so loath was he to inflict upon himself and them the pain of an explanation, if one day, within a week of that time, the notary had not bade his clerk dine with him on the morrow. It was a holiday, and as Carlotta was at home, making ready for the marriage, Tonelli consented to take his place at the table from which he had been a long time absent. But it turned out such a frigid and melancholy banquet as never was known before. The old notary, to whom all things came dimly, finally missed the accustomed warmth of Tonelli's fun, and said, with a little shiver, "Why, what ails you, Tonelli? You are as moody as a man in love."

The notary had been told several times of Tonelli's affair, but it was his characteristic not to remember any gossip later than that of 'Forty-eight.

The Paronsina burst into a laugh full of the cruelty and insult of a woman's long-smothered sense of injury. "Caro nonno," she screamed into her grandfather's dull ear, "he is really in despair how to support his happiness. He is shy, even of his old friends, —he has had so little experience. It is the first love of a young man. Bisogna compatire la gioventù, caro nonno." And her tongue being finally loosed, the Paronsina broke into incoherent mockeries, that hurt more from their purpose than their point, and gave no one greater pain than herself.

Tonelli sat sad and perfectly mute under the infliction, but he said in his heart, "I have merited worse."

At first the signora remained quite aghast; but when she collected herself, she called out peremptorily, "Madamigella, you push the affair a little beyond. Cease!"

The Paronsina having said all she desired, ceased, panting.

The old notary, for whose slow sense all but her first words had been too quick, though all had been spoken at him, said drily, turning to Tonelli, "I imagine that my deafness is not always a misfortune."

It was by an inexplicable, but hardly less inevitable, violence to the inclinations of each that, after this miserable dinner, the

signora, the Paronsina, and Tonelli should
go forth together for their wonted promenade
on the Molo. Use, which is the second, is
also very often the stronger nature, and so
these parted friends made a last show of
union and harmony. In nothing had their
amity been more fatally broken than in this
careful homage to its forms; and now, as
they walked up and down in the moonlight,
they were of the saddest kind of appari-
tions,—not mere disembodied spirits, which,
however, are bad enough, but disanimated
bodies, which are far worse, and of which
people are not more afraid only because they
go about in society so commonly. As on
many and many another night of summers
past, the moon came up and stood over the
Lido, striking far across the glittering lagoon,
and everywhere winning the flattered eye to
the dark masses of shadow upon the water;
to the trees of the Gardens, to the trees and
towers and domes of the cloistered and tem-
pled isles. Scene of pensive and incomparable
loveliness! giving even to the stranger, in
some faint and most unequal fashion, a sense
of the awful meaning of exile to the Venetian, who in all other lands in the world is
doubly an alien, from their unutterable

unlikeness to his sole and beautiful city. The prospect had that pathetic unreality to the friends which natural things always assume to people playing a part, and I imagine that they saw it not more substantial than it appears to the exile in his dreams. In their promenade they met again and again the unknown wonted faces ; they even encountered some acquaintances, whom they greeted, and with whom they chatted for a while ; and when at nine the bronze giants beat the hour upon their bell,—with as remote effect as if they were giants of the times before the flood,—they were aware of Pennellini, promptly appearing like an exact and methodical spectre.

But to-night the Paronsina, wno had made the scene no compliments, did not insist as usual upon the ice at Florian's; and Pennellini took his formal leave of the friends under the arch of the Clock Tower, and they walked silently homeward through the echoing Merceria.

At the notary's gate Tonelli would have said good-night, but the signora made him enter with them, and then abruptly left him standing with the Paronsina in the gallery, while she was heard hurrying away to her own apartment. She reappeared, extending toward Tonelli both hands, upon which glittered and glittered manifold skeins of the delicate chain of Venice.

She had a very stately and impressive bearing, as she stood there in the moonlight, and addressed him with a collected voice. "Tonelli," she said, "I think you have treated your oldest and best friends very cruelly. Was it not enough that you should take yourself from us, but you must also forbid our hearts to follow you even in sympathy and good wishes? I had almost thought to say adieu for ever to-night; but," she continued, with a breaking utterance, and passing tenderly to the familiar form of address, "I cannot part so with thee. Thou hast been too like a son to me, too like a brother to my poor Clarice. Maybe thou no longer lovest us, yet I think thou wilt not disdain this gift for thy wife. Take it, Tonelli, if not for our sake, perhaps then for the sake of sorrows that in times past we have shared together in this unhappy Venice."

Here the signora ended perforce the speech, which had been long for her, and the Paronsina burst into a passion of weeping, — not more at her mamma's words than out of self-pity and from the national sensibility.

Tonelli took the chain, and reverently kissed it and the hands that gave it. He had a helpless sense of the injustice the signora's words and the Paronsina's tears did him ; he knew that they put him with feminine excess further in the wrong than even his own weakness had ; but he tried to express nothing of this,—it was but part of the miserable maze in which his life was involved. With what courage he might he owned his error, but protested his faithful friendship, and poured out all his troubles, —his love for Carlotta, his regret for them, his shame and remorse for himself. They forgave him, and there was everything in their words and will to restore their old friendship, and keep it ; and when the gate with a loud clang closed upon Tonelli, going from them, they all felt that it had irrevocably perished.

I do not say that there was not always a decent and affectionate bearing on the part of the Paronsina and her mother towards Tonelli and his wife ; I acknowledge that it was but too careful and faultless a tenderness, ever conscious of its own fragility. Far more natural was the satisfaction they took in the delayed fruitfulness of Tonelli's marriage, and then in the fact that his child was a girl, and not a boy.   It was but human that they should doubt his happiness, and that the signora should always say, when hard pressed with questions upon the matter : "Yes, Tonelli is married ; but if it were to do again, I think he would do it to-morrow rather than to-day."

THE END.

Edinburgh University Press:
T. AND A. CONSTABLE, PRINTERS TO HER MAJESTY.

www.ingramcontent.com/pod-product-compliance
Lightning Source LLC
Chambersburg PA
CBHW020110030726

47498CB00006B/2040